Ellen said, "because my maid assures me that if I must marry, such a man would be full of fun and gig. But you cannot imagine how uncomfortable I feel, Lord Bracknell." She looked wistfully away from him. "I never wanted to marry at all."

He caught her chin with his hand and forced her to look at him. "Every woman wishes to marry. You are lying!"

She slapped his hand away, her eyes blazing. "Why should I tell a falsehood about such a thing? I can see now that you are unsuitable. Good day." Dropping a curtsey, Ellen moved into the entrance hall, wondering what to do next. What if the viscount did not follow her?

But with a thoroughly wicked gleam in his eye, he moved to stand very close to her, barring the exit.

"How tempting you are," he said. He again took her chin, forcing her to look at him, and kissed her. The pressure of his lips was strong, almost insistent. . . .

The Golden Heiress

SARAH MONTROSE

BERKLEY BOOKS, NEW YORK

THE GOLDEN HEIRESS

A Berkley Book / published by arrangement with
the author

PRINTING HISTORY
Berkley edition / January 1990

ISBN: 0-425-11922-X

A BERKLEY BOOK® TM 757,375
Berkley Books are published by The Berkley Publishing Group,
200 Madison Avenue, New York, New York 10016.
The name "BERKLEY" and the "B" logo
are trademarks belonging to Berkley Publishing Corporation.

PRINTED IN THE UNITED STATES OF AMERICA

10 9 8 7 6 5 4 3 2 1

To Dorothy,
for many years of friendship

The Golden Heiress

Chapter One

ELLEN KNEW HER father's solicitor was speaking, for she could see his lips move and could even detect a fine layer of perspiration beaded upon the man's brow, but she could not hear him. He was reading her papa's will on an early day in March of 1812, a circumstance unusual in that Vincent Warfield had been dead for a full six months. This late reading had been his expressed wish, and for her part Ellen was grateful for the reprieve because her father's disappearance in a yachting accident had been a terrible blow to her. She had loved her papa deeply.

But there was something very strange about the will, and for the longest moment her mind refused to listen to the words Mr. Ibthorpe seemed to be stumbling over. And the library at Warfield Hall, where she sat rather numbly listening to her father's bequests, had become filled with the most annoying humming sound. Was she going deaf or merely stark-staring mad?

Lifting a bejeweled hand, she cut off the timid little man and cried, "One moment, Mr. Ibthorpe. I cannot quite make out what you are saying. Would you—" She stopped speaking and realized her own voice seemed to have dispelled the tiresome noise. She settled back into her rose-colored velvet chair and rubbed the rather large emerald adorning the middle finger of her right hand. "Ah, that is much better. But I seem to have missed a portion of the text. Pray begin again where it reads something like *little inclination*, if you please!"

The small-boned solicitor smiled nervously at his deceased client's daughter and gulped. She was quite beautiful as she regarded him from large green eyes, her honey curls in a cloud about her face, but he had felt the effects of her temper once before, having received a nasty cut on the head, and all for having merely entered old Warfield's estate office at a most inopportune moment. Though, to give her justice, she had not meant to hit him with the expensive Sevres vase—she had been aiming at her poor papa.

"If it pleases you, miss . . . " —his fingers trembled as he held the wicked document—"I daresay you had better read this portion for yourself." He set the sheaf of papers on the desk in front of Ellen and bowed to her. "Perhaps when you have perused your father's will, we could discuss any questions you might have. . . ." He walked toward the door and turned to bow one last time to her. He knew he should stand by her in this moment of great need, but odds fish, he still bore a scar from that vase and had no wish to enhance his skull with a second one. "I'm sorry, miss, but I'd better be going. I'll be at the Artichoke until Friday next." And with that he was gone.

Ellen would have tried to detain the man, but he seemed so very set on going. Had she offended him? She could not quite comprehend all that was going forward or why she had been unable to hear Mr. Ibthorpe's voice through that one particular passage. And why, most particularly, did she feel glued to her chair, as though her physical being knew something her mind was as yet unwilling to accept?

Her father's will. Ellen shook her head, still unable to fully credit that her papa was gone. For the first few nights she had cried continually, missing him so enormously, she wondered if she would ever recover. But after a few weeks, every precious memory, and some not so delightful to recall, seemed to float along beside her and ease the pain of so final a separation.

With these thoughts Ellen smiled, her courage somehow returning to her, and she was ready to face the massive document that now lay in a neat pile upon her father's ancient desk. She rose quickly and seated herself upon his leather chair. The smell of a fine soap, his scent, permeated the chair, and Ellen felt somehow that he was with her. But not the sweet, loving man who bought her trinkets and every manner of trumpery, but the stern, unbending father who once flailed her with a strip of willow for having brought her horse in near to exhaustion, lathered and unfed, after a day's jaunt about the North Downs.

Her posterior hurt just thinking about it, and she could almost feel the welts again as she shifted slightly in the chair. The words *least inclination* jumped out at her from the formal document sitting innocently on a green desk pad, and she quickly read the first page. Her heart beat faster with each word, and a horrifying sense that she was caught in the midst of a ghastly nightmare overtook her every faculty. What did he mean that she must marry a man whom her father knew full well she despised?

But there it was! His words were clear, and he had effectually stripped her of her inheritance—that is, unless, she pursued and married Lord Bracknell, a known rakehell and womanizer. And if she did not fulfill this condition, then her fortune, every property she had cherished since she was a girl, every diamond, ruby, and pearl, every beloved horse in the well-stocked Warfield stables, would go to her cousin and brother-in-law, Ambrose Hazeley.

And she would not marry Bracknell, not for a thousand fortunes!

Her eye caught sight of the sparkling emerald ring she wore nearly every day. A Warfield jewel, a ring her mother had worn. Even this heirloom would be given to Ambrose should she fail to bring Lord Bracknell up to scratch. How could her papa have done such a cruel thing to her?

Ellen reread the document, dwelling heavily upon one quite uncomfortable portion enumerating several of her faults: ". . . given your temper, your caustic tongue, and spoiled manner of throwing fits whenever you do not have your way . . . not to mention your rejection of every suitor I ever paraded before you . . ."

Papa had simply never understood her. She did not wish to marry. She had a wonderful independence and did not want it mucked up with a passel of brats and a husband like her sister Celeste's who gamed away her inheritance at Boodle's. And she certainly had no wish to marry that braggart, that worm, that rakehell, Lord Bracknell. She had rather, by far, marry a fish.

Separating this letter from the rest of the will, for it was directed quite personally just to her with the very ironic address "My Beloved Daughter," Ellen rose to her feet and began pacing the long book-lined chamber. Beloved daughter, indeed! Oh, Papa, what have you done? And what did she know anyway of fixing her interest with such a man! He was a hardened gamester who delighted in shocking the ton by flaunting his mistresses in Rotten Row. Rotten Row, indeed!

Reaching the windows at the far end of the room overlooking her beautiful gardens that were just beginning to bud, Ellen suddenly felt very small. A memory, never to be despised too much, struck her mind with such force, she felt the situation to be completely hopeless.

She remembered vividly the first time she had met Lord Bracknell. Emerging from her box at the opera, she had nearly bumped into the viscount, who was heading in the opposite direction at a brisk pace. He had laughed and bowed to her and then decided she was worth at least one careful appraisal through his quizzing glass. And how devilishly handsome he had appeared, standing tall in the candlelight, his black hair brushed carefully in the Brutus fashion, his exquisitely cut black coat of superfine molded to a pair of broad shoulders, his neckcloth in perfect folds, his black pantaloons encasing lean, well-shaped legs. How he had taken her breath away as he regarded her with an appreciative gaze that took in every inch of her royal blue satin gown, dwelling upon its décolletage and afterward slowly examining each feature of her face, much as a connoisseur of art might examine one of Turner's majestic works. And how deep his hazel eyes had appeared, fathomless with a glimmer of amusement lurking in their depths to tease his victims.

She had felt completely lost beneath his gaze for a long moment and certainly too stunned to speak. No wonder he had a reputation among her friends as one who trifled with hearts, for even in this brief exchange Ellen had felt disturbed to the very roots of her feminine soul. But when she had collected herself sufficiently, and considered what a triumph it would be to add Lord Bracknell to her own court, she determined to dazzle him with her smile, just as she had so completely bowled over any number of her beaux. But the moment she had fixed just the right shape to her mouth and precisely the correct degree of maidenly flirtation to her eyes, his own gaze clouded over quickly with a disgust so great, she had wanted to disappear into the woodwork. His expression grew arrogant, his lips positively curled in scorn, and he had wasted no time in snubbing her. Merciful heavens, no one had ever snubbed her before! The memory of it, as she crumpled her father's letter between suddenly violent hands, burned her cheeks even now, a full twelve months later, and she could not keep from stamping her feet on the hard ash wood of the library floor.

Fortunately no one had seen Bracknell give her this silent setdown, and she had been free from what could have been the most devastating joke of the season: the Golden Heiress snubbed by Bracknell.

He was indeed everything she despised, especially since he had so effectively ground her pride into the carpet of the Royal Italian Opera House. She would never forgive him.

And now she must pursue him, like any simpering, useless, silly female, and capture him. The very idea of having to reduce herself to wiles and stratagems again caused her to stamp her feet, which only reminded her of her father's letter, ". . . and spoiled manner of throwing fits whenever you do not have your way." Was she so very bad?

Turning her back on the paned window and smoothing the letter out, Ellen let the morning light flood the missive as she read the contents yet again. She still felt as though she were trapped within a terrible nightmare, but she had only one course open to her—she must enchant Lord Bracknell and somehow persuade him to marry her. Gripping the letter tightly, her mind adjusting moment by moment to the task before her, Ellen quit the library. As she moved into the black-and-white–tiled entrance hall, the demitrain of her silvery gray morning gown billowed slightly behind her.

She entered the expansive drawing room, pulled hard on the bellpull, and waited, her hands on her hips, the letter clutched in her fingers, her bosom heaving with renewed anger. How could her papa have done this to her? She had so much to bear with the management of the estate alone that the idea of having to expend her energies upon pursuing Lord Bracknell was inconvenient in the extreme! Merciful heavens, her world was falling down about her ears!

When the stodgy butler appeared, bowing his bald head to her, she raised the vellum paper toward him and cried, "I am removing to London at once! The entire world has gone mad!"

If Mr. Ewshott was surprised by this announcement, he certainly knew better than to show it and merely nodded. "Of course, miss. At once." He then coughed in a hesitant manner and said, "Begging your pardon, miss, but Mrs. Ewshott is quite feverish to have a few words with you. Something about your father, I believe."

Ellen stared at him, her eyes widening in surprise. Would there be no end to what she must endure? Did Mrs. Ewshott now have some unbelievable news to impart, for she was never *feverish* over anything! In a quiet voice, she said numbly, "Of course. Have her attend me here."

When Mr. Ewshott's footsteps faded away, Ellen turned to face the richly appointed drawing room where ancient tables and curios of mahogany gleamed from liberal applications of turpentine and beeswax, and scattered bowls of lavender potpourri combined to lend a fresh, clean fragrance to the chamber. Several chairs and sofas covered in rich forest green velvets and flowered chintzes presented an elegant, bright appearance, and delicate Sevres china, mirrors in leafed gold, books bound in fine calfskin, and golden candlesticks arranged throughout were the final adornments to a room where Ellen had seen the better part of her two and twenty years.

The room spoke to her suddenly, as though begging her not to go, reminding her of moments from the past with her mama when she was ten, music lessons with an austere governess, concealing herself behind the drapes when the Prince of Wales, now Regent, had come to visit papa. What a week of preparation that had been, with Cook nearly out of her senses until her father had hired a French chef to relieve Cook of the burden of trying to please the Prince. Warfield Hall was her home, her father's home. The place where her mother had died of a sudden fever. Hadn't her father realized that so hardened a gamester as Lord Bracknell would no doubt ruin the Warfield fortune? Hadn't her sister's scandalous marriage to a gamester proved to her papa just what would happen were she to marry someone cut from a similar cloth as Ambrose?

She had always thought her father the most clever of men, scheming and conniving and laughing. But this? Surely he had gone mad in his last few weeks of life. Surely!

And then the thought occurred to her that, though she must marry Bracknell, he need never see Warfield Hall. She could make certain all of the extensive property was bound to their children or to her own nephews. And she felt a certain measure of relief, her confidence again returning to her. With diligence she was sure she could work out each of these miserable details and not have to suffer too dreadfully. But how was she to win Bracknell in the first place?

Easing into a chair by the massive fireplace of Kentish ragstone, the only remnant of the ancient hall that bespoke a lineage that went as far back as the Conquest, Ellen shaded her face with the letter. How was she to win Bracknell when he so clearly disapproved of her? Had Ambrose been an honorable man, a man capable of managing the properties, she might have refused to comply with the will on principle alone, with the thought that her sister, Celeste, who had married Ambrose, might have enjoyed the benefits of being mistress of Warfield Hall. But unleashing Ambrose Hazeley upon the Hall would have been akin to letting the fox into the henhouse. He had gone through her sister's fortune, forty thousand pounds, in the first three years of their marriage. Such were his propensities. And Bracknell, from everything she had ever heard of him, was quite as bad. No. She had no choice but to fulfill the conditions of the will.

The blood rushed to her face as she considered Ambrose. How horrified she had been to learn from her sister's pale lips that he was deeply in debt and that only Dower House, where Celeste resided year-round, had kept up an appearance of solvency. Forty thousand pounds, lost at Boodle's, White's, Watier's, or possibly at one of the private gaming establishments notorious for relieving either the very green or the very reckless of an entire fortune in one night.

And poor Celeste. She had loved Ambrose, but now she had nothing but her connection to Warfield Hall. Ellen was in the habit of giving her sister pin money every quarter and of sending the dressmaker to take her measurements whenever she had dresses made up for herself. She also saw to the needs of her nephews—two ungovernable children, particularly by Celeste's weak hand, who were wild to a fault, and a terror to Mr. and Mrs. Ewshott, who generally found the little darlings walking the parapets three stories above the graveled drive when they came to visit.

Her face still shaded, her thoughts full of Celeste and Ambrose and Bracknell, Ellen did not hear the housekeeper's approach and jumped in her chair as Mrs. Ewshott said "Miss Ellen, I do be sorry to disturb you." She was not a refined woman by any means. Her speech was plain, her face round and ordinary, but she was a born manager, and kept a staff of thirty, as well as her husband, who enjoyed nipping at the cooking wine, under the strictest control.

She thrust something wrapped in a linen kerchief toward Ellen. "I have felt as though I have kept the master's ghost here, carrying this about with me day and night. And he told me he was set on your having this, should he up and die suddenly, shaking his finger at me while he spoke, frowning at me from under them bushy gray brows of his, so I was afeard I'd fail him. And he wanted you to have it on the same day as the reading of the will. And when he told me he would come back to haunt me, and bring my first husband back with him, well, I needn't tell you I've been nigh sick to death with worry, besides looking over my shoulder whenever so much as a breeze ruffled my bonnet! Please take it, miss, and I'll thank ye kindly."

As Ellen took the small object, she heard Mrs. Ewshott heave a sigh of relief, and glanced up at her. She seemed oddly pale. Ellen unwrapped the kerchief and could have laughed for the suspense Mrs. Ewshott's recital created in her, for it was only her father's gold snuffbox, a little dented in places, especially on the top, where a series of minuscule leaves edged the fairly plain box. Certainly her papa had overemphasized the importance of the task. "But I don't understand. You mean my father charged you with giving this to me on a specific day? And he told you this before he died? Why? I don't understand?"

"I don't know, miss, but that determined he was—six months to the day, he said."

"How very strange. Did he say anything more to you? I mean . . ." —her voice broke as thoughts of him suddenly filled her mind—"was it very long before . . ." —she took a deep breath and met the housekeeper's concerned gaze—"before he disappeared at sea?"

Mrs. Ewshott pinched her lips together and jerked a kerchief from the long sleeve of her black bombazine dress. Dabbing at her eyes and sniffling, she finally said, "'Twere a fortnight only. I thought he was in his cups, to be sure, when he spoke of dying and seeing that his old snuffbox was given to you. But he gave no appearance he'd been drinking any more than what was usual with him." She blew her nose. "And he told me only what I have told you—that I was to see you got the snuffbox."

Ellen leaned back in the chair, rubbing her fingers across the dented leaves on the lid, and said, "Thank you, Mrs. Ewshott. I cannot imagine what my father could possibly have meant by this unless he simply didn't want me to forget him, if ever I could!"

"No, miss. If ever any of us could. He was certainly a tough master, but fair. And quite handsome except for those bushy brows."

Ellen looked up at her and smiled. "Yes, except for his brows. I always thought he had the look of a wild boar."

Mrs. Ewshott cocked her head slightly and agreed. "Yes, a boar. I'd not considered it afore, but you've the right of it." She folded her hands primly across her black skirts and dropped the smallest curtsy. "Mr. Ewshott says you'll be removing to London, and I don't wish to be bothering you, so I'll attend to my duties now. If you need anything, you just send for me, Miss Ellen. I—I wish the master hadn't stuck his spoon in the wall when he was at such a playful age, for a more frisky man you'd never want to see, but you've done well by all of us and by the Hall and we're glad you're mistress here now, though it's been a sad time for you."

Ellen still fingered the gold box, her heart heavy with missing her father, her sensibilities considerably bruised by the conditions of the will. But a scheme fixed itself in her mind: she would find Bracknell, court him by every means fair or foul, marry him, and if she found her life with him completely unbearable, she could lock herself away at Warfield Hall forever.

Ellen rose to her feet, the kerchief slipping from her gray silk gown to the thick burgundy carpet beneath her feet, her hands holding both the will and the snuffbox tightly. "Thank you, Mrs. Ewshott. You've been a great help to me, and we have brushed through quite well, haven't we? But on to London. I have pressing estate business there. Will you be so good as to send Becky to me?"

Mrs. Ewshott wiped her eyes one last time and immediately bent down to retrieve Ellen's kerchief. Just as she handed it back to Ellen, the most startling squeal, followed quickly by a tremolo of giggles, rang clear to the domed ceiling of the entrance hall and resounded through the drawing room.

Both ladies grew rigidly still, expressions of wide-eyed horror suffusing their faces, as they cried in unison "Becky!"

Chapter Two

MRS. EWSHOTT SAID, "I should have let her go the first time, the minx! 'Tis all my fault."

Ellen saw that her housekeeper was preparing to do battle as she straightened the cuffs of her gown in turn. Laying a hand on Mrs. Ewshott's lean arm, she said, "Wait! Let me speak with her. She is, after all, my abigail, though why I permitted her to stay after you found her in the buttery with one of the footmen, I shall never comprehend!"

"She's bewitched us all!"

Ellen set the letter and the snuffbox on a table by the sofa and, moving beyond Mrs. Ewshott, hurried to the entrance hall, where she heard a great deal more giggling issuing from the library. How unconscionable of Becky, who had been her maid for a little over a year, to conduct her flirtation in one of the main rooms of the Hall!

Flouncing toward the closed doors of the library, she heard Jack's husky male voice and felt a slight blush suffuse her cheeks. Pausing before the carved oak doors, uncertain for just a moment whether she should proceed or not, Ellen decided that this time Becky had gone too far. A tryst with one of the younger grooms, and in her library! Becky most certainly would have to go.

Thrusting the doors open, her green eyes flaming, Ellen swept into the long chamber where less than an hour earlier Mr. Ibthorpe had stood nearly shaking in his boots as he read the will. But there before her now was Becky, bent slightly backward as Jack, his powdered wig askew, nibbled in a hungry fashion upon her neck.

Becky did not at first see her mistress, and Ellen was far too shocked at the manner in which both man and woman were caught up in their reprehensible dallying to say anything at first. She stood rooted to the rose-colored swirls of the Oriental rug and watched in mute fascination at the terribly forward manner in which the young man was easing his lips down that very tender portion of skin below the ear. Ellen placed a hand at her own throat as though the deed were being done to her. How she shivered at the thought. Would Bracknell do such a thing? Decidedly he would revel in it!

When Becky finally did perceive her mistress, she gave a loud squeak and thrust the footman away. But this young man was by no means willing to let his little mudhen slip away so easily and he tried to gather her up in his arms again only to be kicked forcefully in the shins. It was not until then he realized Becky was going through some rather strange motions as she curtsied, her freckled face a fiery shade of red, her lips moving in a series of "I do be sorry, miss. I do be sorry!" Whatever did his pet mean by such odd ways? he wondered and then he saw Ellen. Horror ripped through him at the sight of the mistress of the house who had once given him a severe dressing down for merely smiling at Celeste—well, perhaps he had winked at her. His eyes rolled back in his head, and without a single thought to his pride he lost all consciousness.

"Lord, ha' mercy, he's done fainted dead away!" Becky cried. "What a cawker!"

Ellen regarded first Becky and then the crumpled form of the footman, and then Becky again. When she found her voice, she said, "I shan't ask you what you were doing, for I daresay you would give me such a recital as to put me quite to the blush! But, Becky, how could you, when you have been warned time and again by Mrs. Ewshott and myself? And here! In the library! Could you not at least have had some imagination and proposed the barn or one of the other outbuildings? There is a charming dovecote scarcely used anymore just inside the home wood, for instance."

Becky appeared contrite as she bowed her head slightly, but Ellen perceived a smile lingering on her lips and was not surprised when she said, "I hadn't thought of the dovecote!"

"Becky!"

Heaving a sigh and bowing her head further still, Becky dipped another curtsy and muttered, "I do be sorry, but Percival here," and she gestured down to the prone footman who had lost his wig completely, "has the sweetest ways." She then glanced at her lover, and with a calculating frown on her freckled brow she continued, "Although he ain't got a backbone to speak of."

Surprised, Ellen said, "I thought his name was Jack. I remember last week, when Mrs. Ewshott found you in the buttery, she said you had been, er, flirting with Jack."

Becky shrugged, "I found out he was a thief, Miss Ellen, for he had took three bottles of claret and that's why he were always taking me to the buttery. Mr. Ewshott threw him from the gates not three days ago. I was a bit sorry at first, but I never could abide anyone who would steal from his employers." She nodded fiercely, then sighed. "But I expect it all turned out quite well, for I wouldn't ha' met Percival otherwise. And I hope you won't 'old this against him, Miss Ellen! 'Twere my fault he came into the library. I done teased him so!"

"That I don't doubt," Ellen said, wondering how it was her anger over the situation seemed to slowly fade away with every word her quite promiscuous maid uttered. Becky had indeed charmed everyone.

Appearing quite remorseful as she moved to a long cherrywood sofa table, Becky said, "I hope you won't turn him off, miss. He's worked here nigh on eight years. 'Twere my fault entirely." And as though she owned Warfield Hall, Becky lifted several yellow daffodils from their vase, flowers Ellen had grown in her succession houses, and dipped a hand into the water. Her fingers now wet she replaced the daffodils, then hurried back to her dearest

Percival and flicked water over his pale features.

Ellen watched Becky with something akin to admiration, for she was never ruffled even in the most scandalous of situations. Sitting down in the rose velvet chair, she wondered what to do with her maid as Becky dropped to her knees beside her latest beau and gently slapped his face.

When Percival awoke from his unconscious state, he nearly went off again until Ellen reassured him that though he had behaved badly, she would overlook his iniquity if he would but show a little more constraint with regard to the female servants, and especially with Becky!

Percival was quick in his assurances and vowed he would not so much as cast one eye at Becky Lovedean ever again. But then he looked up into Becky's face with such longing that Ellen could only shake her head in wonderment. What was it these young men saw in her rather plain abigail? What mysterious spell had she cast over them that they were willing to risk their employment, even their futures, over her? Becky was gap-toothed, her smile wide and sensual. Her hair was dressed in a mass of frizzy red curls over which she wore a very small white cap, tied beneath her chin with green satin ribbons. Her eyes were a sultry amber color, perhaps her best feature, but beyond that, Ellen could only shake her head—her face was round, her skin heavily freckled, and her nose somewhat flat. What was the secret of her charms?

Percival finally found his feet, and after retrieving his wig, he bowed with a red face to Ellen and left the ladies alone. Ellen commanded her maid to follow her and was silent until they reached the privacy of her bedchamber. Regarding Becky with a stern expression, she said, "You have been warned repeatedly about your flirtations. You know what this means, don't you?"

Becky nodded, "Aye, miss, but his kisses are that sweet!"

Ellen regarded the twinkle in Becky's amber eyes and tried not to be swayed again by her maid's cozening smiles. It was too late now. Becky was no longer to be trusted. A tryst in the library had quite put her beyond the pale.

"Becky, I will have to let you go." She felt quite the meanest creature on earth as she uttered these words and turned sharply away from the stricken, anxious look that flickered momentarily in her maid's eyes. Ellen crossed the room to stand beside her dressing table and stared out the window at the neatly scythed lawns and beyond the gardens to the home farm. Bracknell would ruin such a fine piece of property. She sighed. She did not wish to give up Warfield Hall. And she did not wish to give up Becky, for she had a remarkable ability to dress her honey curls. "You must see there is nothing else I can do. If I permitted any of the servants such liberties—"

She fingered the perfume bottles on her dressing table, letting the silky pink fringe on one run through her fingers and glanced back at her maid only to find Becky's amber eyes apprehensive.

Smiling halfheartedly, Becky said, "I don't see as I blame you, Miss Ellen. From the time I was first become a woman, I couldn't keep away from the likes of Jack or Percival. And I was sorry to hear the gardener's son had left to enlist in the army. His kisses were a bit of heaven." She winked. "I am a wicked sinner, just as Mrs. Ewshott says. Ain't no denying wat is plain to everyone." She dropped a small curtsy, and in a tight voice, still keeping a smile on her face, said, "I'll pack me bags now if ye like."

Ellen watched her maid turn away, and she wondered if Bracknell had ever dallied with the likes of Becky. Most certainly he had. Certainly Becky could have charmed the likes of Lord Bracknell. Certainly!

And just as Becky put her hand on the brass doorknob Ellen cried out, "Wait! One moment! Of course! Becky, forget everything I have just said. But of course! Why did I not think of it before. You are precisely what is needed in this most despicable situation! You are to come to London with me. Oh, I am so glad I thought of it. Why, who better to instruct me on how to capture a rake than you?"

She felt so relieved and excited at the same time that she

ran to her maid, pulled her by the arm, and whirled her once about the room. "Providence has sent you here! I know it. Becky, you shall save me from poverty!"

Becky pulled away from her mistress and eyed her warily. "Have you gone daft, miss? What do you mean, poverty? Surely you've enough brass to last a hundred lifetimes!"

Ellen shook her head, "Only if I'm able to make a certain viscount fall in love with me and marry me! I'll be impoverished otherwise. You must help me! Indeed you must! You must teach me everything you know."

Becky's eyes gleamed in a purely wicked fashion as she said "Everything?"

Ellen blushed at the implications of her maid's words and responded shyly, "Well, not everything I suppose. Just enough to make Lord Bracknell fall head over ears in love with me."

Becky frowned. "Bracknell? Lord Bracknell? That cove what was here not a fortnight afore yer father died?"

Had Becky struck her hard across the face, Ellen would not have felt the impact of her words more intensely. Finding herself near her ancient Elizabethan chair covered in a lavender damask, Ellen fell into the soft cushions and asked, "What do you know of Bracknell? How could he have been here without my knowing? Are you certain it was Bracknell?" She now felt some conspiracy was at work, and a sense of despair took hold of her heart. Had the two men conspired together against her? Was Bracknell now expecting her to come to London and make sheep's eyes at him?

Becky shook her head. "'Twas so long ago, in the stables. But I'm sure it was Lord Bracknell. I heard him and the master talking to the head groom. And I had just a glimpse of him, too. I was in the loft with, er, well, never mind, but I couldn't resist just peeking over the edge. He saw me, too, though to his credit he never said nothin' to your papa." She pressed a hand to her cheek. "I shook all night afeard I'd be turned off without a reference. I owe him, I do, and he was so terribly handsome and built lean and strong. Mayhap I be mistaken, but if it be Bracknell, you'll have a hard time bringing that one up to scratch!"

Ellen again regarded her maid in wonder and shook her head from side to side as though dazed. Becky was certainly shrewd, and she could not resist asking, "But can it be done, Becky? I mean with the right sort of smiles and gowns and mannerisms, can I ever hope to win such a man?" She could not bring herself to mention the episode at the opera.

Becky nodded, a smug smile on her wide lips as she said, "Anything is possible, miss, and after all, Bracknell be only a man like all the rest—pulling his boots off one after t'other!"

When a mountain of baggage had been assembled in the long entrance hall, Mr. Ewshott flung the front door wide. The sounds of a brisk traveling chariot and a lumbering fourgon crunching along the drive evoked in Ellen a growing sense of immediacy, as though every moment spent in Hampshire was one less she had to accomplish her task.

Pulling her blue kid gloves on, she reviewed Becky's efficient list of all she would need to take to London, and afterward informed Mrs. Ewshott which household tasks had not been attended to as well as to whom notes of regret should be sent canceling a variety of engagements. Her heart was racing at the prospect of leaving, her mind fixed on London, when the shouts of two little boys assailed her ears. Oh, no! Her nephews Marcus and Julian and certainly her sister, Celeste. A delay of no mean order!

"Auntie Ellen! Where are you going? London! Take us with you," the boys cried as they peeked their heads into the entrance hall. They apparently had little hope of being invited to go, for they merely smiled in response to Ellen's greeting of "Hallo, scamps!" then dashed backward down the stone steps to review the magnificent horses and coaches now waiting in the drive.

The boys immediately attacked the equipage, leaping in and out of the carriage, shouting at the grooms, patting the horses, and teasing one of the footmen, who tried to whisk them away with frowns and shooing motions, to no avail. Ellen shook her head and wished her sister had more control over her sons. And just as this thought passed through her mind, Celeste appeared at the bottom step and in her pacifying manner cried, "Now, my little darlings, be very good while I speak with your Auntie Ellen. There's a dear, Julian! Stop kicking the servant. Why don't you take Marcus around to the stables?"

"But, Mama! You know Auntie has forbidden us—"

"Nonsense. Your aunt is far too strict; now do as your Mama bids you."

Ellen would have taken the situation in hand had she not been pressed to leave. As it was, she saw her nephews cast triumphant expressions in her direction and tear off toward the stables. She would have to give Huntley an extra guinea for the torture he would now have to endure.

"Ellen, dearest," Celeste said as she crossed the threshold, her hands tucked into a sealskin muff against the cloudy March skies. "Why did you not tell me you were leaving? Are you going to London so soon? I thought you had planned on staying here through Easter?"

Ellen nodded, and would have explained, but her sister regarded the large leather-strapped trunks with great longing and continued, "I have not been to London in ages, and oh, how I wish I could go with you. And why must Ambrose forbid it?"

Ellen felt torn. She wanted to help her sister, but she desperately needed to leave. Greeting Celeste with a kiss on her cheek, she said, "I'm afraid a rather urgent matter requires my immediate attention, and though I wish we could have a comfortable coze, I must leave as soon as possible." She looked at her sister in a hopeful manner, but without effect.

Celeste did not want Ellen to go and regarded her sister with large tears welling up in her light blue eyes. At one time she had been pretty and lively, her fair complexion blooming with a healthy glow delicately tinting each cheek. But after six years of a very trying marriage, her eyes did not sparkle as much as Ellen wished and some of the color had disappeared from her cheeks. She wanted to see Celeste happy and radiant again, which she was upon occasion when a mysterious poet would send her his latest worshipful sonnet, but her happiness was never long of duration—she was too far removed from the society she loved.

"Don't cry, Celly! Pray do not—"

"It is just that I am so miserable when you are gone."

"I have no choice but to go." Ellen glanced about the hall, at the footmen now busily carting the baggage to the fourgon. Mrs. Ewshott stood discreetly by, and with silent gestures made clear to the servants which bags should go next. Becky, she could see from the corner of her eye, had taken this timely interruption to make her way outside and begin a flirtation with one of the footmen whom she felt certain was Percival's older brother, Tristan.

Ellen returned her attention to her sister. "I suppose I could put off going for a few minutes while we have some tea. I had meant to stop by Dower House; truly I had. But the business is dreadfully urgent." She thought of the condition of the will, and her stomach turned over completely. A month seemed like no time at all to try to win Bracknell's affections! "And I greatly fear I will be gone three or four weeks."

"But that is nearly a month!" Celeste cried.

Ellen requested Mrs. Ewshott to bring some tea into the drawing room. Unbuttoning her pelisse, she lead her sister into the chamber where they had once played duets on the harp and the pianoforte. "Until I saw Mr. Ibthorpe a few hours ago, I had no intention of going. But now I must! You cannot imagine—" She broke off, wondering whether she should say anything to her sister of their father's will and then decided against it.

Celeste removed her pelisse of burgundy merino and sat on a chintz sofa near the fireplace. She sighed deeply, her sad azure eyes fixed on the blazing fire, and said, "I had two creditors call upon me at Dower House this morning. They came all the way from London hoping to see Ambrose."

Sitting down on her favorite green chair, Ellen could scarcely credit what her sister was saying. She was horrified and exclaimed, "No! Impossible! Surely your maid sent them away. Who permitted these men into your house?"

"They discovered me in the garden. I was never more surprised or mortified." Retrieving an ice-blue kerchief from her reticule, Celeste dabbed at the tears tumbling down her thin cheeks.

"Dearest, you should not have been mortified! You have done nothing wrong, nor have you done anything to be ashamed of! And most certainly you should have sent them about their business! Or sent them here. Ewshott would have taken them down several pegs before they so much as removed their beaver hats."

Pressing her handkerchief against her trembling lips, Celeste said, "But these poor men both have very large families and . . . and one of them said his wife was dying of the consumption. And then I have not seen Ambrose in months! And to have these gentlemen descend upon me . . . " A sob caught in Celeste's throat, and Ellen immediately moved to sit by her younger sister and slipped an arm about her shoulder.

Cradling her as though she were a little girl, she said, "There, there, Celly. Don't cry. I shall think of something. You should not have to bear this burden. Your husband's debts have nothing to do with you."

"I know, but what am I to do?" Then her mood changed quite suddenly, much as a child's would. Giving Ellen a bright little push, her face wreathed in smiles, she cried, "I almost forgot! I am not entirely full of bad news! Look!" And she pulled a letter from the depths of her muff. "My admirer has written another sonnet in honor of my beauty. Listen to how this one begins: '*Oh goddess of tresses fair and light*.' You must read it. It is so much like Milton!"

Ellen rose to her feet, her hands clasped tightly together, her gaze fixed upon her sister, "Celeste, what are you thinking? You cannot continue encouraging him."

"But he amuses me! And I am sad too much of the time. Even you have said so."

"I know, dearest. But what can come of it? You are married, with two fine boys . . . "

Lifting her chin, Celeste said, "I would not be the first female to . . . to have her own cicisbeo. In London, I understand it is quite fashionable and the gentlemen recline at your feet and compose all manner of poetry and worship the color of your eyes . . . " She appeared in that moment to be exceedingly starved for affection, and Ellen's heart went out to her sister yet again. Celeste had married Ambrose when she was only a silly chit of fifteen—nearly seven years ago. But in all that time she seemed to have gained little more understanding from her mistakes than a wet goose.

Celeste continued, "And my *admirer* loves me, and I think I may be falling in love with him, and oh, Ellen, it is the sweetest sensation in all the world!"

Ellen scarcely knew what to say as she began pacing the carpet. "Things have progressed this far? I had no idea. Celeste, you are not thinking of—you cannot be considering another elopement?"

Celeste placed her muff behind her head and leaning back on it, stared up at the ceiling, "I don't know. When I am with him—"

"You have seen him? Celeste, who is this magical poet?"

She tilted her head to regard her sister. "I will tell you only this: do you remember that very brief excursion of ours to Bath last summer, and the afternoon you were laid upon your bed with a headache?"

Ellen nodded.

"I met him at the pump room, but I will tell you no more, for I see you mean to scold me."

"Do I know him, Celly?"

"I believe you would know him if I spoke his name, which is why I will not. But he is not a particular friend of yours, and I know for certain you have never danced with him."

"But where have you met him so secretly? Not one word has ever been bandied about in our drawing rooms, nor one morsel of gossip ever touched my ears! And you know what some of our neighbors are; if they had even the slightest suspicion, I should have heard nothing else for weeks!" Ellen regarded her sister in amazement.

Celeste smiled shyly as she plucked at a row of lavender bows adorning her muslin walking dress. "I have met him only twice, I promise you, and he was so gentlemanly . . . a true friend!" She laughed softly, her eyes shining. "Do you remember the ancient dovecote in the home wood, all trailing with vines, and bramble, and in the summer it is covered with yellow roses?"

Ellen pressed her hand to her cheek. "I have a faint recollection of it," she said, remembering with great irony her reference to it less than an hour earlier.

At that moment the housekeeper appeared with the tea tray, and for her part Ellen was grateful. She did not wish to hear more of Celeste's poet. She had her own difficulties to attend to, and the mere thought that her sister might be involved in an affair showing every promise of fast becoming a dreadful scandal sent a shiver down her spine.

After they had each taken a cup of tea and Mrs. Ewshott's black skirts had disappeared into the entrance hall, Ellen said with a hint of exasperation in her voice, "Pray, tell me no more. Only promise me you will not lose your head over this poet of yours. At least not until I have returned from London, and then you may be as foolish as you wish, for I shall be here to keep your heart in line."

The radiance on Celeste's face dimmed just as quickly as it had come, and she said, "If only Ambrose had loved me but a little. I know I was very young when we married, but he truly seemed to have an affection for me, or at least I thought he did. And how is it I can still feel an attachment to him after being ignored for years?"

Ellen spoke quietly. "Ambrose has always possessed a certain charm, and I believe he did love you, as much as he could. But anyone who had such a doting mother would achieve adulthood uncommonly spoiled. 'Brosy, my darling, you've dirt on your coat and breeches!' And what else were little boys to be doing but romping through the woods? 'Brosy, dearest, there is a hint of rain in the air; you should stay before the fire, and I will read to you.' When I think of his mama, truly I could forgive him anything; that is if he had not made your life such a misery!"

Celeste nodded her head slowly. "I daresay it is not entirely his fault. But what is to become of him? He is deeply in debt, and when he pesters me to ask you for money, I know he is trying to drain off the Warfield fortune through me. And there are moments, when his eyes grow very dark, I feel he would do anything to possess the Hall." She shivered slightly as she sipped her tea, and in a quiet voice added, "His mama was forever telling him he had been cheated from his rightful inheritance."

After a moment Celeste replaced her cup and saucer on the silver tray and cried, "Oh, never mind. I will fall into a fit of the dismals if I dwell upon Ambrose a moment longer." She stood up quite suddenly and, tucking her hands into her muff, said, "And you must be going, mustn't you? I expect Huntley will be coming in here at any moment, carrying on about his horses and how you have kept them standing about in the wind!"

Celeste was such an odd mixture of woman and child that from one moment to the next Ellen did not know what to expect from her. And after several hugs, as though she would not be seeing Celeste again for a year, Ellen finally climbed into the traveling coach and waved good-bye to her sister and to a very muddied pair of little boys whose mouths were stuffed full of chocolates.

And within a few minutes, with Becky seated beside her and waving furiously to Percival, Ellen took a last glimpse of Warfield Hall and wondered if she would still be mistress there in a month's time. As the coach bowled down the avenue of lime trees, her mind was still full of Ambrose and Celeste and her poet. And as a light spring rain began pattering the roof of the carriage, Ellen felt a heaviness descend upon her heart. A few hours ago life had been sweet and full of every promise. Indeed, in a year, when she had grown more comfortable with her father's death, she had planned to take a trip to the West Indies. She smiled slightly as the coach hit the rutted lane beyond the gates and began a slow, swaying progress toward the macadamized road near the village. How scandalized her London acquaintances would have been by such a scheme! And she would have done it regardless of what anyone might have said to her. She was the wealthy Miss Warfield, and as her papa had said times out of mind, a fortune was its own code of conduct.

Why, she could even hear the tittle-tattle: "She's off to the Indies now. Merciful heavens, she has a screw loose that one, just like her sister who eloped with Ambrose Hazeley. The whole family's for Bedlam!"

The pleasant sensation these few thoughts evoked quickly dissipated in the face of her present scheme with Bracknell.

She felt sudden tears burn her eyes. How swiftly life had changed for her. She felt in her reticule for her kerchief, an unusual white linen handkerchief embroidered in gold thread, which her father had given to her nearly seven months ago. It seemed like only yesterday.

He had brought the kerchief back from Portsmouth just before he died and had made a present of it to her. She dabbed at her eyes, the gold thread of the embroidery a little harsh against her delicate white skin. "Gold embroidery and her golden hair," he'd said. She remembered how he had touched her hair in that moment, caressing one of her curls and appearing quite sad. Did he know he was about to perish? Had he experienced some foreknowledge of his demise?

As Ellen leaned back into the squabs, returning the precious kerchief to her reticule, she thought she had never looked upon a visit to London with such misery.

Chapter Three

ON THE FOLLOWING morning Ellen sat in Lord Bracknell's library alone, her heart sitting in her throat. She was waiting for the viscount to appear, hoping it would be soon, but determined to wait the entire morning if necessary, in order to catch him completely off guard.

She had pushed her way into his house, under the disapproving eye of what she immediately sensed was a corruptible butler, and announced she had an appointment with his lordship at nine o'clock. She assured the thick-necked retainer, her smile at its most dazzling, that the viscount was fully aware of their little assignation and, thrusting two gold guineas into Mr. Mytchett's outstretched hand, told him with lifted chin there would not be the least need to announce her. She would await his lordship in the library! If she heard a certain sniggering as the man walked away, biting into his newfound fortune, she ignored it.

Straightening her back, Ellen practiced yet again precisely what she would say to the viscount and listened intently for any sound of his imminent approach. It was nearly ten now, and her nerves were raw to disintegrating. What if he did not awaken until noon? Then she would simply have to wait; she must wait! Surprise was the very essence of this attack. How else was she to completely bowl him over?

Becky had dressed her hair with great care, threading blue satin ribbons throughout her gold curls. She wore small diamond drops upon each ear, and for the hundredth time she pinched her cheeks slightly and nibbled at her lips hoping to enhance their rosy color.

The brass clock upon the mantel now chimed ten. She had waited an hour, and butterflies again assaulted her stomach. If only he had not been quite so handsome, she would undoubtedly have felt she had more of the upper hand. But above all she dreaded the very distinct possibility he would remember her from the opera and throw her from his town house in disgust. She leaned forward in the gold velvet chair and kicked her feet. Lord have mercy, she did not believe she could bear much more. Would he never arise from his bed of lechery and drunkenness?

And then she heard an odd slapping sound issue from the grand, marbled entryway, and her heart quickened to an alarming pace. Someone was in the entrance hall! She leaned her head to catch the first view of whomever it was, for it could just as easily be one of the footmen or even one of the maids as Bracknell. She swallowed hard. Footsteps.

Oh, lord what was she doing here, in Lord Bracknell's library? For just a moment she wondered, given his reputation, whether she would even escape with her virtue. She must be very careful.

It was he! His tall figure darkened the doorway, and Ellen rose quickly to her feet, clutched her sable muff to her bosom, and waited for him to discover he was not alone in his library. He was every bit as handsome as she remembered. She could not go through with this! He would think her the most forward of females! He would search his mind for a certain occasion at the . . .

"Lord Bracknell?" she asked quietly as he caught sight of her and stopped in his tracks. He looked sufficiently astonished, and she felt a little confidence return to her, "Oh, dear," she said in what she hoped was an apologetic voice. "I have been greatly deceived! You will not do at all! I have been sent upon a fool's errand."

Lord Bracknell, that Go among the Goers, had entered his library both barefoot and in a state of considerable undress, with only a long burgundy brocade dressing gown, albeit tied sturdily about his waist, covering his tall, manly form. He had been in the midst of a yawn, running his hands through his thick black hair when he saw her. And though she looked familiar, he wasn't quite certain who she was.

Frozen in his tracks, his head splitting from the effects of three bottles of exquisite claret served up at Boodle's on the evening before, he thundered, "Who the devil are you? And what mutton-headed, cork-brained idiot permitted you into my house!" These last words, shouted over his shoulder, were intended to bring his butler running. Instead the hallway was silent, and his temper had effectually released so sharp a pain stabbing every square inch of his brain that he bent over slightly and stumbled to the doorjamb, where he propped himself up for a moment. Emitting a loud groan, he moved gingerly to an Empire-style chair, where he sat down and dropped his head into his hands. "Hell and damnation!" he muttered, his eyes squeezed shut.

Casting her muff onto a sofa of dark brown velvet near the fireplace, Ellen crossed the room quickly and gave the bellpull several firm tugs. She regarded him with a considering expression, trying to remember all the unique advice Becky had given her: "And should he be needing something for the headache, just be the one to see that he gets it! The gentlemen do love to be cosseted a bit. Only don't bruise his pride too much. They be quite delicate when it comes to being manly."

Her voice low and caressing, Ellen addressed the viscount. "I daresay your evening was a trifle bosky?"

He glanced up at her and nodded, a puzzled frown on his face.

She opened her eyes wide, much of her fear sitting quietly for the moment at the pit of her stomach. "And I take it you did not receive my letter, for you appear entirely ignorant of our appointment?" She hoped he did not notice how her fingers trembled as she pulled a curl that rested on her shoulder. Becky had told her to touch her hair whenever she could, to keep drawing his eyes to her face, to her hair, to the satin ribbons wound through her honey curls.

Lord Bracknell, resting his head in his hands, again squeezed his eyes shut, as though he wished she would simply disappear, and said, "I never make arrangements to meet young ladies, however beautiful, at ungodly hours of the morning."

Ellen felt a twinge of excitement tickle her heart. He thought her beautiful. This was at least something. "My lord!" Ellen cried. "I beg to assure you it is well past ten o'clock. It is hardly the break of dawn. And I had almost given up hope–especially when your butler looked so disapproving when I told him you were fully aware of our little assignation."

He lifted his head to gaze at her and again frowned. "What the devil do you mean by our 'assignation'? I don't even know you." And just as he said this, some little bell went off in his head. He did know her, or at least he had seen her before. And there was something about her expression, her features, that put him forcibly in mind of someone he knew quite well. "Have we met? Do I know you? If only my mind weren't quite so fuzzy."

Ellen shook her head, her curls dancing about her face. "I met you once years ago when I was still in the schoolroom." She watched his face intently. "You knew my father; indeed, I understand you were with him shortly before he died. My name is Ellen Warfield."

He sat bolt upright in his chair, his physical discomforts nearly forgotten at her words. Good god, he had not expected this! But neither had he expected Vincent Warfield's death six month's earlier.

He rose suddenly, feeling her grief acutely, for he could see it written on her face. Seizing both of her hands in his own, he cried, "My dear girl! I am so sorry."

Ellen could not have been more shocked or overwhelmed if he had thrown cold water in her face. His sympathy was sincere and completely unexpected. She drew back from him, a thousand emotions pummeling her at once–sudden memories of her father, her dislike of Bracknell and all that he stood for, her intense desire to keep him at an emotional distance, her anger at her father for writing such a ridiculous will.

Bracknell released her hands, puzzled by the expressions that crossed her face one after another. So it has begun, he thought. He turned away from her, and a memory flooded his mind, an evening at Drury Lane–or was it the opera house? Yes, the opera–of a beautiful girl, and her simpering smiles, and his disgust.

As he turned back suddenly, Ellen knew what he was remembering, and she felt a blush creep up her cheeks. Would this interview never end? And why had she pulled away from him? Becky's advice on this point had been very specific: "Never draw back, miss, unless it be to tease him a little." None of it would work. He was too much for her, too handsome, too debauched, too understanding. But she must try, or she would lose the Hall. Hoping to correct her error, she said, "You are very kind, Lord Bracknell. I miss him very much."

"I am sorry," he murmured, as he watched her face, intently. And then he saw it. Vincent had trained him to see such things. It was a faint expression only–a sharpness in her green eyes. The chit was trying to cozen him. But why? Was this Warfield's doing? The navy office in Portsmouth had told him to wait six months after the old man's death for new instructions. Was Ellen here to deliver them? Or did Warfield's schemes go deeper than that? And what had Ellen meant by saying he would not do?

Ellen felt uncomfortable as she met his piercing hazel eyes, and a little shot of fear ran down her spine. His expression was critical, appraising, he was every bit as shrewd as her father.

She felt an odd breathlessness as he dug deeper into her soul, his gaze searching, penetrating. Was this how he entrapped the women in his life, by staring at them, by trying to unravel their thoughts, their intentions, before ever a word was spoken?

His eyes were a little hooded, his cheekbones high and pronounced, his jaw strong, his nose straight. The slight stubble covering his chin served merely to enhance his masculinity, and Ellen now felt she could not look away from him even if she wanted to. He was holding her gaze simply by the force of his will. And then the piercing look faded slightly to be replaced by a lurking smile, and his voice touched her with its low, seductive tones, "And why, Miss Warfield, will I not do, as you so cruelly put it?"

"What?" Ellen asked, forgetting for a moment she had uttered these words earlier. "Oh, that! Yes. Well." He finally released her gaze, and she was able to look anywhere but into his hazel eyes–at the hard ash floor, at an odd assortment of small tools upon his desk. Her gaze rested on them for a moment. So he prepared his own snuff, just like her father.

Clearing her throat, she was about to answer his question when the butler interrupted their tête-à-tête, bowing politely and begging to know his lordship's wishes.

Ellen remembered Becky's advice and interposed quickly, "Please be so good as to bring your master a large tankard of your very strongest ale."

Mr. Mytchett, his small blue eyes fixed upon Lord Bracknell, stood completely motionless waiting to receive an affirming nod from his master. He was never one to forget, no matter how generously the female had greased his palm, on which side his bread was buttered. When the viscount nodded to him, he bowed low and quit the room.

Lord Bracknell regarded Ellen with an approving smile. "You are a female of uncommonly good sense. Of course, I would expect as much from Warfield's daughter. But why, my dear, have you risked your reputation so thoroughly by crossing the portals of this den of iniquity?" And he gestured in an expansive manner about him.

"Then you did not receive my letter?" she asked, her eyes wide. She knew his attitude toward her had shifted slightly, particularly since he had addressed her in so familiar a fashion, but she was not certain how or why.

He shook his head, crossing his arms in front of him as he continued to regard her in his appraising manner.

Ellen said, "I explained my predicament most carefully

in the letter I sent to you at least a fortnight ago. I cannot imagine what happened to it!" She felt breathless, lying so brazenly, but she ignored her feelings and plunged on. "At any rate, my father mentioned three prospective husbands in his will, and my maid, Becky, who had seen you several months ago, assured me you were quite suitable since I desired to marry a rake. I have a strong preference for rakes."

"For what?" He sounded genuinely shocked.

"For rakehells, my lord. You are a rake, are you not?"

"No! Yes, that is; I had never considered it. I do not take part in orgies, if that is what you mean, nor do I drink wine from skulls."

Ellen took a small step backward, shocked at his words, for she had never really considered what sort of things a man of rakish propensities might engage in and did not wish to pursue the subject any further. She prattled on, hoping he did not see her discomfiture. "As it happens, my father left a . . . a quite difficult condition to his will, which I only discovered recently, and the short of it is that I must marry in a month's time or forfeit my entire fortune to my cousin Ambrose." She gulped. Bracknell was so very astute, she would not have been surprised if he had pulled her blond curls and forced her to tell him the real truth. But she knew if she told him her father had named him specifically, he would have dismissed her with a jerk of his thumb toward the door. She did not want him to read any more of her thoughts, so she dropped her gaze to regard his toes. They were funny-looking, with curly hairs, which gave his bare feet a rather wrinkled appearance. Suddenly he did not seem so awesome a figure, and she looked up at him and smiled.

As he met her amused green eyes, he thought for a moment he had just stepped into the most enchanting dream. Good god, but she was beautiful and so intriguing! How much of what she was telling him was true and how much was Warfield's doing? He said, "Your father left such a condition in his will? Then I am truly sorry for you. It must be most uncomfortable."

She met his concerned gaze and could not resist confiding in him a little. With a sigh she said, "You cannot imagine how uncomfortable, Lord Bracknell. I never wanted to marry at all." She looked wistfully away from him. "It was such a fine independence, too."

He caught her chin with his hand and forced her to look at him. "Every woman wishes to marry. You are lying!"

She slapped his hand away, her eyes blazing. "I would never tell a falsehood about such a thing. Why should I?"

"But you have lied about some things. Admit it!"

Her nostrils flaring, she said, "I will do what I have to do in order to preserve my inheritance. I didn't wish it this way."

"How very like your father you are, but I still must know why I 'will not do'? And why you wish to marry a rake?"

Ellen turned away from him and tried for a lighter tone, hoping to distract him from his terrible scrutiny. How was she ever to bamboozle him if he kept her so completely off balance. "I fear I will offend you, sir, but I will be blunt. I wish to marry a rake because my maid, Becky, assures me if I must marry, such a man would be full of fun and gig. As to why you are not suitable, the case is simple." She looked at him over her shoulder and with a wave of her hand said, "You've no precision of eye. Look at you! Your hair is hither and yon, your dressing gown is lopsided, and . . . and you've curly hairs on your toes! You are not at all fastidious enough for my exacting tastes." She retraced her steps to the sofa and retrieved her muff. "In his will my father named two other gentlemen for my consideration." She pulled a slip of paper from her muff and read the names. "One Jeremy Andover and a Mr. Laurence Chawton. I have every intention of visiting them in their rooms today as well, although Becky tells me neither is quite of so rakish a disposition as you." She shrugged, hoping to appear as though she meant to accept her fate, and continued. "Time is a very pressing matter, you see." She smiled faintly. "I cannot afford to observe the proprieties as much as I would like to, and I am sorry I have wasted your time. Good day."

Dropping a very brief curtsy, she moved into the entrance hall, wondering what to do next. What if the viscount did not follow her? Certainly she had made a complete mess of the entire interview. She was too easily angered, too susceptible to his expressions of concern, and still too furious at the conditions of the will to have done anything but make a great muddle of it.

But Lord Bracknell was fully intrigued by her. He remembered a simpering miss from the opera, but now he realized he had judged her too quickly. She had depths that surprised him. But what was her game? he wondered.

"I won't permit you to leave yet, Miss Warfield. You have wounded my pride. And your censure is by far too harsh. Can any man appear to advantage in a dressing gown?" And he held his hands wide, that same quirky smile softening his hazel eyes.

Ellen scanned him from head to foot and thought no man of her acquaintance had ever appeared to such advantage and was spared answering him by the timely arrival of Mr. Mytchett, who bore a gleaming silver tankard. After presenting the ale to Lord Bracknell, he asked quietly, "Was the young lady leaving?"

"Yes." Ellen answered as she moved to stand by the door.

"No!" Lord Bracknell countered with a firm shake of his head. "She is not leaving. I have not finished with her." With a raised brow Mytchett took this as his cue to depart. Bracknell drank deeply from the tankard and then set it on an inlaid table by the staircase.

With a thoroughly wicked gleam in his eye, he moved to stand very close to her, placing himself in front of the door, barring her exit. Smiling into her eyes, he took her chin in his hand, kissed her gently on the lips, then regarded her steadily. "So, you wish to marry a rake. How very singular, but I should inform you in general such men rarely become leg-shackled, even to the prettiest of females."

"I am exceedingly wealthy," Ellen teased.

He laughed, "Madame, you grow increasingly desirable, and almost I wish I were of the marrying sort."

Ellen tried to keep her emotions at bay, but his lips had been incredibly tender and though the taste of ale remained, she found his kiss a very sweet, pleasant sensation. "Then *all's well that ends well*, for I know we should not suit."

Bracknell smiled. "How you tempt me. And such a direct challenge! However, may I at least suggest I help you in your difficulties? I happen to be very well acquainted with the gentlemen you just mentioned and with a little judicious flirting on my part, the day might be won."

"So, you think you could accomplish so much? How very conceited you are!"

He ignored this thrust and said, "I should be delighted to get up a little party to Vauxhall–a masquerade, of course." He slipped an arm about her waist. "Wafer-thin slices of ham, the smoothest of champagnes, delectable creams . . . but I wander from the point." He reveled in the dazed expression on her face. What an easy prey she would be, yet she was Warfield's daughter. How his conscience pricked him. "I am certain Jeremy and Laurence would be delighted to make your acquaintance. They are both of them in urgent need of heiresses, as it happens!"

"How provoking you are! Would my fortune be my only charm, then?"

"Your last of many. A cloud of angel hair, emerald eyes, and the loveliest lips I have importuned in a very long time."

She swallowed hard, finding his hazel eyes again reaching into her soul. No wonder he had a reputation for destroying the feminine heart. He was an unconscionable rogue! Did he know the effect he was having on her? Of course he did, drat the man. "A masquerade at Vauxhall? I'm not certain . . ." She looked away from him, trying to break his spell, so she might be able to think more clearly. But this was a mistake, for he again took her chin, forcing her to look at him, and kissed her a second time. But the pressure of his lips was stronger this time, almost insistent. Ellen felt her heart race at his rather frightening ability to command her, and then he pulled away from her slightly, while still holding her fast.

In a low voice, as though he were sharing a secret, he said, "You shan't care for Jeremy at all. He is by far too romantic and poetic a figure for you. And as for Laurie, his bent is strictly intellectual. But they are both of them rake-hells, though only in a noble sense, and would certainly fill any of your vacant hours with 'fun and gig.' Vauxhall?"

To Ellen's ears, he sounded mocking, but of the moment she didn't care. She only wanted him to kiss her again. How truly reckless she felt, but hadn't Becky told her to enjoy his kisses if she possibly could? Lord in heaven, what an easy task that had become!

She leaned into him. "You are very kind to offer your services, and I will not be so missish as to refuse them. You may flirt with me all you like!"

And then he kissed her so hard, she could scarcely breathe. Part of her felt panicky and wanted to run away from Lord Bracknell, to retreat from his town house and pretend she had never come to his home in the first place. He frightened her. But another part of her welcomed this onslaught to her sensibilities. He was taking her away from every painful thought of the past few months into a misty world of everything bright and wonderful. Her heart, which had for so long seemed like a weight within her breast, now felt free. In a moment of insight Ellen realized, as he held her in a firm, strong embrace, that in his arms, she felt very, very safe.

When Ellen was carefully tucked into a hackney coach and returning to her town house in Berkeley Square, she tried very hard to forget Lord Bracknell's kisses. She could not afford to have her schemes overset even the slightest degree, and the viscount's astonishing ability to wreak havoc with her emotions only convinced her she must be carefully guarded with him. And if he believed he would never marry, then he understood very little about Ellen Warfield. She was, after all, her father's daughter.

Chapter Four

ON THE FOLLOWING morning Ellen sat before a mahogany *secrétaire* at the far end of the drawing room, her gaze fixed for the moment on a wall clock of carved bird's-eye maple. She watched the relentless second hand tick past each roman numeral and felt somehow that her entire life was attached to it. She had so little time, after all, to attach Lord Bracknell to her side, and the task seemed impossible.

At least Becky had been instructing her carefully in all manner of dalliance, but where was her maid anyway? Ellen had summoned her nearly twenty minutes earlier, but as yet Becky had not attended her. Was it so very much to ask, she thought with irony, that her own abigail respond in a timely fashion to her summons? And she wondered yet again if she had been so very wise in retaining Becky Lovedean.

Giving her gold curls a toss, Ellen returned to the task at hand. She was busy scribbling a list of duties she had left but half attended to when she had so hastily quit Warfield Hall, and the scratching of her pen along with the relentless ticking of the clock were the only sounds in the long, well-appointed receiving room. She felt like Papa's watch when it had been wound a little too tightly. Even her handwriting suffered. She tried to read several of the words, she had just written and found it impossible. Dipping her quill into the silver inkwell, she struck the bottom of the jar with such force that she ruined the tip. Heaven help her, she was as useless as her absent maid. And where was Becky?

Wrapping the quill carefully in a linen rag, Ellen swallowed very hard as she watched her fingers actually tremble. Setting the wrapped quill on the desk, she realized her nerves were very close to snapping, and Becky was only a small part of her worries. The entire morning Lord Bracknell's image had stolen time and again into her mind. Never in her entire life had she experienced anything so unsettling as his kisses, and the truth was she longed for more. No wonder Becky judged the value of the men in her life by how they kissed. If such were the only measure a woman could apply to a man's worth, good heavens, Bracknell was surely worth her father's entire stable of racing horses. What a deplorable comparison, she thought with a rueful smile, and picked up a new quill.

After a few minutes Ellen heard the door open, and she twisted around in her chair, expecting to see Becky and fully prepared to upbraid her for her tardiness. She was surprised to find not her own abigail, but the timid face of a young undermaid, whom the other servants had nicknamed Twitty.

The diminutive servant peeked around the doorjamb and squeaked, "Miss Warfield, I do be sorry to disturb you, but I've a message for you from Becky."

"Pray, come in," Ellen called to her in a gentle voice, for the maid seemed quite distressed as she finally took two steps into the room. She was a rather homely, thin girl of no more than fourteen summers, her cheeks drawn and her brown eyes puffy in the dim morning light of the long chamber.

The maid dipped a curtsy, her head bowed slightly, her right hand clutching a handkerchief. "I was to tell you Becky's gone out, miss—shopping in New Bond Street for the costume you was wishing for this evening—and, and that you was not to worry." Twitty then lifted her kerchief to her eyes and wiped them brusquely.

Ellen did not know what to make of her maid's distress and asked, "Twitty, what is wrong? Is Becky ill? Has there been an accident?" And with a smile, eyeing her maid teasingly, she said "Or has she perhaps been flirting with the footmen again."

And much to Ellen's surprise, the young girl promptly burst into tears. "That she has, miss, but I dinnit mean to speak of it to you, at least I meant to, but I never meant to become a watering pot!"

Ellen went to the servant immediately and begged her to sit down on a small, ladder-back chair by the *secrétaire*. "Now, what is this? So many tears over a mere footman?"

The girl, who had been blowing her nose, wiped it suddenly, and lifted her chin, appearing quite affronted as she said, "Weren't a *mere* footman. 'Twere *my* footman. And George is so very handsome, save for his ears what stick out from his head like two butterfly catchers, and until that female, that is, until Becky came here, we was nearly engaged to be married, me and George. She's a sly one, Becky is, and you should see how she cuts a wheedle with all the menservants, and even Mary what is married to the third footman is like to tear Becky's hair out, every last frizzy red curl that she has!"

Ellen found it nearly impossible to be sympathetic with the maid's difficulties, but she did think it unkind of Becky to be trifling with Twitty's beau. She would speak to her maid, and said as much to the young undermaid, but did not hesitate to add, "And I'm certain, however, that if *your* footman has formed a lasting passion for you, then he won't let his head be completely turned by Becky."

Twitty did not seem completely convinced and, after blowing her nose again, dipped a small curtsy and added in another squeak, "Of course, miss." After shifting in her seat several times, she added, "And I would be ever so grateful if you did not speak of the matter to Mrs. Sparsholt, for if she knew I'd come in here and spoke to you of Becky, why, she'd turn me off without a reference." She then leaned toward Ellen, her forehead puckered, and said, "And there be something else what I think you ought to know. Just afore Becky left so sudden-like to find you a costume, I seen her get this letter, on very fine paper. And

I never seen a body turn so white as fast as she done when she read the letter. 'Tweren't queer that she got a love billet, for all the maids do now and then—those what can read, like me, for instance—but that was when she decided to go out for your costume, not afore you rung for her, 'twere after! And I thought you should know, for she seemed quite fidgety and nervous-like!" And she nodded several times, her brown eyes squinting in a very knowing fashion.

Ellen thanked the young maid for her forthrightness, promised to keep mum with the housekeeper, Mrs. Sparsholt, and sent Twitty away if not actually smiling, then at least able to dry her tears. Once the maid was gone, Ellen returned to her chair, sitting down very slowly and wondering with much trepidation just what devilment Becky was engaged in.

Lord Bracknell tugged gently upon the folds of his cravat, effecting the difficult pattern known as the *trône d'amour*, and finally nodded his head in approval. Declaring the task complete, he held out each of his arms in turn to receive his blue riding coat. He never dressed hurriedly, but ascribed to Brummell's mode of simplicity and care.

Mr. Huntspill, a very quiet, stoic young man with a straight posture and precise manner of speaking, nodded his approval as well. He had served in the capacity of Lord Bracknell's valet for nearly two years now and felt his master was just as every gentleman should be—not affecting the dandy and everything of the first quality, from the fine weave of his linen neckcloths to his top boots by Hoby. And after struggling to help his lordship into his boots, working up a film of perspiration on his own brow, Huntspill carefully buffed the gleaming leather, and addressed a small matter the butler had brought to his attention earlier.

"Mr. Mytchett received a letter for you, my Lord, just a little past ten." He cleared his throat, for he was not certain just how much he needed to tell the viscount and finally said, "A serving person delivered it to the front door—a female servant, as it were." Mytchett had described the female as gap-toothed with red hair and a very bold manner of speaking, but Huntspill did not feel his master would wish to be informed of such trifles.

Lord Bracknell took the missive and regarded his valet with a hint of a smile on his lips. The missive no doubt was from Ellen. How very much he had enjoyed kissing her on the day before. He lifted the billet to his nose and sniffed. What an odd fragrance, almost like soap.

All his senses became focused in that moment. No love billet this. He tore it open and just as he read the first line, he knew it was from Vincent. Vincent!

But it was dated six months prior. Damn and blast! Had he been informed immediately, he would have sent someone after the servant.

"Huntspill, who brought this missive? Why was I not informed immediately?"

The valet froze in the act of collecting several discarded neckcloths, and felt his own cravat constrict his throat. "I don't know, my lord. Mr. Mytchett frowned over the entire episode being extremely disapproving of the female using the front door, and I had no idea it was of significance. Should I ring for Mytchett? I am sorry, my lord."

Lord Bracknell waved a hand of dismissal. "No, I suppose it is of little use now. Did Mytchett say anything else of her?"

"Only that she was rather gap-toothed and pretty, though her face was quite freckled. He meant to send her around to the servant's entrance, but she called him a stiff-rumped fool, thrust the letter into his hand, and returned to her hackney coach."

"Stiff-rumped? I daresay Mytchett will be on his high ropes the entire day."

"As to that, I cannot say, my lord," Huntspill responded in his dignified manner.

But Lord Bracknell saw the faintest smile touch his valet's lips and sent him away with an admonition to avoid Mytchett if he could.

When the valet had shut the solid oak door behind him,

Lord Bracknell sat down before a bureau-bookcase of burr walnut and spread out the letter. And as each word surmounted the next, his horror grew with each word he read for the task ahead involved Ellen to an alarming degree. Leaning his head on one hand, he considered his new directives. Vincent had made it clear Ellen possessed three articles he had given to her six months ago, each of which contained false information of supposed national importance, articles that were not only coded but believed to be destined for Wellington himself—a gold-embroidered kerchief, a telegraph fan, and one of Vincent's old snuffboxes.

It was Bracknell's duty, as a servant of His Majesty's Government, to somehow manage surreptitiously to obtain the articles from Ellen, for in so doing he would be assured of flushing out a suspected traitor among the *beau-monde* —good god!—a personage well-known to Ellen. Vincent instructed him to accomplish the task by whatever means he could, and it was this portion of Warfield's letter that disturbed him the most, for Vincent was rather callous in the treatment of his daughter's sensibilities. "And flirt as much with Ellen as you like," he'd written, "for I am convinced it would do the girl a world of good. She has something of a heart of steel, which I daresay even your practiced flirtations could not touch." What a taunting remark. "But if she does happen to fall in love with you, let her down gently, m'boy, gently for my sake. I am off to the Isle of Wight for a holiday. Fair sailing weather tomorrow. Good luck." The letter was almost challenging, as though old Warfield had been daring Bracknell to make Ellen tumble in love with him.

What was Warfield's game? he wondered. First, the truly despicable conditions to Ellen's inheritance, and now this—throwing them both together as if . . . Bracknell leaned back in the maroon leather chair and considered the workings of Vincent's mind. If Warfield expected him to offer for Ellen, then he was an old fool who should have known a great deal better than to try to force his hand. He was sorry for Ellen, but he had no intention of marrying a female of her stamp—quick-tempered and managing and no doubt hunting for a title like every other female of his acquaintance.

Bracknell felt with a little care, once he had actually acquired the articles from Ellen and discovered the identity of the suspect, he could eliminate her from the proceedings entirely. If nothing else, he was concerned for her safety. Bracknell knew from experience that any man so desperate for the ready as to resort to selling his country's secrets would have little hesitation in dispatching anyone standing in his way.

The remainder of the instructions did not really include Ellen. After he had the fan, snuffbox, and kerchief, he was to flaunt them at several private gaming establishments in the West End, and once the suspect had made himself known, he was to proceed directly to Portsmouth, where he would be given new instructions. He whistled suddenly as he read the last paragraph, for it assured Bracknell that the suspect, a known gamester, would eventually betray himself—it had already been carefully put about that the articles were worth fifteen thousand pounds to the bearer, an incredible fortune. And with such stakes, certainly the traitor would do everything he could to gain the same articles from Ellen. But why hadn't Vincent told him the suspect's name? Why so much secrecy, unless Warfield wanted to be very sure such a personage was truly involved in traitorous activities. If the war office or the navy office in Portsmouth were mistaken, and a false rumor began circulating, no amount of public apology could make up for the scandal that would ensue.

Bracknell trusted Vincent to know what he was doing. They had worked together for ten years now, and not once had the old man ever been wrong. But it chafed Lord Bracknell greatly to read that Vincent had also found it necessary, in order to give the viscount the appearance of being a gamester in need of funds, to circulate a second rumor to the effect that Bracknell had mortgaged Three Elms. *Three Elms*. His family's country seat for seven generations. Anyone who knew him would know it to be the the grossest falsehood. Why, he was as devoted to his estate as Ellen Warfield was determined to preserve her inheritance. Yet, however much it went against the grain, he could see Vincent's wisdom. When the suspect learned Bracknell was vying for possession of the articles, such a rumor would corroborate his need for the fortune their sale would bring.

But the very thought of mortgaging Three Elms distressed him so much that he immediately ordered his favorite mount and rode to Hyde Park. There he galloped all over the extensive bridle paths to the cheers of a troupe of unruly boys playing at ducks and drakes in the Serpentine.

By four o'clock in the afternoon, Ellen was ready to scream with vexation, for Becky had still not returned from her little shopping expedition. Surely it would not have taken her maid the entire afternoon to procure a suitable costume. Surely! She was standing by the escritoire, staring down at the completed pile of correspondence, when she heard voices below and then footsteps on the stairs. Becky!

But as the door opened, she was dumbfounded to see, not her maid, but Ambrose, who had not set foot in her town house in over a year. "Cousin," she cried, completely astonished. And how very much he had changed over the years. At one time, he had appeared as any of hundreds of young gentleman who had come to London for the sole purpose of acquiring a little town bronze, sporting Weston's coats, frequenting Jackson's Boxing Saloon, and regularly attending the auctions at Tattersall's.

But somewhere he had acquired not bronze, Ellen thought with a smile, but pink, for Ambrose had become a Tulip among the Tulips, a Bond Street Beau, a Pink of the Ton. And he was so much the dandy, his blond locks pomaded, his clothes in light pastels—he even wore lavender gloves—that Ellen could never see him without experiencing a great shock.

Ambrose lifted his quizzing glass to scan his cousin from head to foot. "Still wearing the willow in your grays, m'dear? But then, you always were singularly fond of your papa." His voice carried an insufferable tone that never failed to irritate Ellen.

"And you are still wearing your pinks, I see," she countered. "Tell me, has Brummell approved this latest costume of yours? I should love to hear his raptures." Ambrose was dressed in a florid manner, sporting a pink satin coat, a yellow-flowered waistcoat, and a lavender nosegay—a veritable sprig of fashion. She watched with great delight as her cousin turned a very dull red, and she smiled with satisfaction.

He bowed, acknowledging a hit and strolled into the room. Taking a chair by the fire, he crossed his legs and said, "You always were made of a very fine mettle, Cousin dearest. But I don't mean to quarrel with you."

Ellen did not want him to stay and could not imagine why he had come, except perhaps to try for the hundredth time to extract money from her. She crossed the room and sat down on a settee of ice blue brocade and said, "I hope you do not mean to detain me very long. I have come to London on a matter of some import, and every moment for the next few weeks is fully engaged."

He smiled suddenly, and Ellen had the strongest sensation that, given his curly blond locks, wispy and weblike, and the long gangly appearance of his limbs, she was staring at a spider.

"Oh, I know all about it," he said in his lazy manner. "You've come to play the hoyden, to ruin your family's honor, to seduce Bracknell."

Ellen knew her mouth had fallen open in a most unbecoming fashion, but she could scarcely credit her ears as she stared very hard at her cousin. Did he know the truth? But how could he? Surely the only two people who knew of her intentions were Becky and her father's rather hen-hearted solicitor.

He laughed lightly delighted now in her discomfiture, but not once did he take his eyes from her. They were unusual green eyes, flecked with slivers of gold. "How does the shoe fit, my lovely Ellie."

"I don't know what you mean, and you know I despise that nickname."

"Of course. Why else would I use it? But tell me how is it I have become so unwelcome in your house? Surely you have time for me. And I came only to warn you against my lord Bracknell and also to remind you of what the ton expects of its little darlings." He drew off a lavender glove and wagged a finger at her "You mustn't visit bachelors—especially unattended even by your maid—in their own homes." He clicked his tongue. "How came you to do such a shatter-brained thing? I should hire a companion for you if I thought you would accept one." He glanced down at the gloved hand and smoothed out a tiny wrinkle.

Ellen felt her heart pause slightly. Had he seen her emerging from Bracknell's town house? When she stepped onto the flags, she had seen only a hackney across the street, but it had not been inhabited by Ambrose, nor by anyone else whom she recognized.

What would happen to her if the *beau monde* discovered her misdeed? Would the patronesses of Almack's then rescind her vouchers? Her cousin was correct. Most assuredly the haut ton would not hesitate to give her the cut direct.

"There, there," he cooed. "I have made you very upset, and I shouldn't tease you, but really you are of an age to know better. One of my own bosom bows—you remember Budgy, don't you? A very decent fellow though quite an opium-eater—well, he saw you emerging from Bracknell's town house, and he promised to remain silent, but whatever does this mean? Are you engaged to the viscount? If you are, I think I should warn you, Cousin dearest, that Bracknell's debts are nearly as large as my own." He sighed. "But then, that would most assuredly explain his interest in you—faith, what a fortune you possess, my dear! I only regret I let a rather foolish, fleeting infatuation persuade me to marry the wrong sister. What merriment we could have enjoyed, you and I. Ah, well, enough of regrets. I just wanted to pass along to you the very interesting *on-dit* that Bracknell has just mortgaged Three Elms."

Ellen could not help herself and exclaimed, "His country seat?" She pressed her hand to her cheek. Good gracious! A libertine and a confirmed gamester. What had her father been thinking? "Oh, no!"

Ambrose lifted his brows and exclaimed, "Why, you surprise me, Ellen. Can it possibly be that you have fallen in love with one of our more notorious rakes?"

"No, of course not." Ellen responded with an impatient jerk of her hand. As soon as the words were out, she wondered how wise she had been. Her cousin eyed her intently, and she felt compelled to explain. "Lord Bracknell was a friend of my father's, and I can't think why Papa would have consorted with such a person. But the fact is there was a . . . bequest in Papa's will, something my father wished Lord Bracknell to have . . . "

What coy words these were, when she was referring to herself. She broke off, her gaze shifting from the suddenly eager expression on Ambrose's face to the fireplace and then to the mantel where a large portrait of her father, quite fitting in size, dominated the room.

Her father stared at her, one bushy brow raised, a smile of mischief dancing on his lips, his eyes full of vigor and strength. Why had he felt it so very necessary to disrupt her life so completely?

Ambrose interrupted her thoughts. "Something for Bracknell in the will? How very intriguing. I am all agog to know what, precisely." Opening a large, ornate snuffbox, he carefully took a pinch and lifted the scented concoction to his thin nostrils, sniffing delicately.

Ellen lowered her gaze to her hands and noticed that a spot of ink had stained her middle finger just above her emerald ring. "It is nothing, really. Nothing of significance. And the truth is I cannot for the life of me comprehend the intricate working's of my father's mind."

Ambrose spoke quietly, "It was not perhaps that old antique snuffbox of his? The gold one?"

Ellen frowned as she recalled Mrs. Ewshott only two days ago, standing nervously before her and presenting the very same box to her. A slight shiver traveled down her back. "No. Why ever would he want to give that to one of his friends?"

Ambrose shrugged, "I always thought it quite charming, and I wouldn't mind in the least possessing it myself." He smiled faintly.

As Ellen regarded her cousin, his long fingers tracing the gold filigree of his own snuffbox with a tender motion, she realized his eyes were inordinately bright as he stared back at her. "I begin to understand you," she said, pausing for a moment to see how her words would affect him. She was satisfied at his suddenly conscious look. "You wish to know if you were mentioned in the will. All this hinting about Papa's snuffbox! Did you hope he had left such an article to you that you might sell it before his will had even been read through? As if my father would leave you anything. He despised you more than I ever did, if that were possible!"

Ambrose returned his snuffbox to the pocket of his coat, then put his glove back on. He spoke lightly, "No, I suppose he would not have bequeathed me even a farthing." And he laughed, as though he had enjoyed robbing Celeste of her dowry.

"Undoubtedly he felt one fortune was sufficient for you," she responded dryly.

"Take care, Cousin; you sound quite bitter." He dusted the sleeve of his coat with his hand and continued: "Good Heavens, I seem to have gotten some of this wretched snuff on my coat sleeve. Have you a kerchief I might borrow?"

Ellen spoke sweetly. "No, I have not. I'm so very sorry." Rising to her feet, she continued, "And if you've no concern larger than the welfare of your coat, I bid you good day." She bowed to him ever so slightly.

He rose to his feet, again adjusting his gloves, "Ah, where have the civilities gone? I wished only to welcome you to London. I don't suppose you have an extra hundred guineas lying forlornly about, do you?"

Ellen hoped her expression reflected the depth of her

feelings as she glowered at him. Apparently it did, for he merely bowed to her and moved toward the door.

In a final parting shot, he said, "I do hope you intend to guard yourself against Bracknell's debauchery. He is a known rakehell, m'dear. No female, especially the beauty you are, is safe from his ploys. And because I could not bear to have a dear cousin of mine plunged into a scandal, I shall swear Budgy to secrecy. It is his job, you know. He works for our government in a very sensitive position at the war office." He pressed a finger to his lips and delivered a very delicate *shushing* sound. "But I can see you need a little looking after, and I mean to keep an eye on you."

He turned to leave, and as he crossed the threshold he collided with Becky, the large bandbox jutting out in front of her catching Ambrose in the chest. The dandy landed squarely on his posterior, and Becky cried out, "La, but I'm that sorry. I didn't see you, Mr. Hazeley!" The bandbox had flown apart upon the collision and a wispy white gown, made from a very gauzy muslin, lay in a heap on the carpeted floor, along with a long band of gold.

Becky moved quickly to help Ambrose right himself, and he began to rebuke her for her clumsiness when he caught sight of the gown and reached down to retrieve it from the carpet. He held it up to look at it and frowned. "Good god! Where did you get this? Why, if I am not mistaken, it is the gown that has become the most scandalous *on dit*. Ellen, are you to wear this? Do you know what it is called and for whom it was created?"

Ellen had crossed the room the moment Becky collided with her cousin, and as she took in the outrageous costume, she felt a blush creep up her cheeks, and she pressed her hands to her face. "Becky, what is this?"

Becky frowned at Ambrose and quickly took the confection from his grasp. Turning to Ellen, she held it against her bosom and let out a very dramatic sigh of pleasure. "If only I were to wear such a delectable costume. Oh, the gentleman what I could attach to me side." She shook her fiery red curls and smiled somewhat stupidly at the gown.

"Twere meant for Harriette Wilson, but never you mind. When the dressmaker discovered the golden heiress wanted it, though I swore her to a vow of silence, she gave it to me without a single batting of her daylights, saying she'd rather you wore it than that hoity-toity cyprian. It's called The Nymph!"

Chapter Five

LATER THAT EVENING Ellen stood before the tall, gilt-edged looking glass in her bedchamber and blinked several times at the shameless image staring back at her. Where was the innocent young miss who planted flower-beds and saw to the mending of the linen every spring? She did not recognize the female in the mirror, and furthermore, she wanted nothing to do with her.

"A trollop!" she cried at last, her emerald eyes wide with horror. "Becky, I cannot wear this costume. Papa would never have permitted me to do so. Why, there's scarcely enough muslin here to make up a kerchief. And—and I have never shown so much bosom in my entire life!" She took a deep breath, and with a shake of her golden curls, unable to credit that she had actually donned the atrocious costume, added, "And surely Lord Bracknell will set me down as a very improperly behaved young lady!"

Several candelabras burned brightly in Ellen's bedchamber of lavenders and pinks, and a thick pile of glowing coals in the fireplace warded off the ever-present chill of the spring night. At the moment, Becky could not answer her mistress because she had three pins compressed between her lips. She was busily taking several tucks at Ellen's minuscule waist, since Harriette Wilson, so it appeared, was considerably higher in the flesh than Miss Warfield. Becky gingerly removed the pins from her mouth, secured them to a black silk ribbon dangling from her waist, and said, "Nay, Bracknell will most like be so bowled over he'll not think about how improper it is until after the reading of the banns, and then he'll like to forbid you to wear the gown ever again, what hypocrites men are!"

Becky's back ached from working furiously over the costume for the past hour, and she straightened up, stretching her arms over her head. She was bone-tired. Besides having traipsed into two-dozen shops along New Bond Street in search of The Nymph, Becky had found it necessary actually to lie to Ellen in order to convince her shopping had been her only activity of the day. And there were moments, however well Vincent had trained her, when telling whiskers did not come easily. And after Ellen had accepted the sincerely spoken falsehoods, Becky had begun an even more fatiguing process—persuading her mistress to wear the quite scandalous costume. Only after she had set the maids to converting Ellen's fur-lined domino of black silk to a stunning gold cape—so her mistress might remain both warm and partially covered the entire evening—did Ellen finally acquiesce.

But now, as Becky made several adjustments to the costume, stitching up a half-dozen small fish here and there, Ellen was again balking at the prospect of wearing The Nymph. Deftly tacking a little dart near the waist, Becky began her arguments all over again. "And have you forgotten the very reason why you be wearing such a costume? You've less than a month to marry Bracknell, and as for your papa, why, if he don't like your costume . . . that is, your papa, God rest his soul, is the one what put you in this terrible fix! So, never you pay no mind to what he might have thought!" And she muttered beneath her breath, "The old goat!"

"What was that, Becky?" Ellen asked, her brow puckered as she turned from side to side before the mirror looking at the offending gown.

"Nought you would wish me to repeat, and do stop fidgeting!"

Ellen sighed. "Do you think I shall enchant Lord Bracknell? Would he fall in love with me merely because of this costume?" She lifted her skirts slightly and stared at the pretty gold sandals with delicate bands, that tied about her ankles. In her heart, she added the very lowering thought and would I want such a man?

"Nay, don't be daft!" Becky cried, as she again straightened her back and regarded Ellen's figure in the mirror. "Only you must trust me a bit. The costume 'tis perfect, and Lord Bracknell will be quite deranged with just looking at you. And mayhap he won't fall in love with you because of it, but I think he'll look harder at you than he's ever done afore. Just make certain you don't blush and simper—unless it be to tease him, of course—rather just hold your head up and give him stare for stare!" Becky bent over one last time to complete the stitching of the final dart, and when she had finished, she removed several remaining pins, adding these to the black ribbon at her waist.

Stepping away from Ellen, she exclaimed, "Aye, but you're that pretty. And one last thing, miss. I've always found if you can saddle a man with one or two articles what are quite personal—a little box, for instance, or a kerchief—then he's like to be thinking of you a bit more often than he would otherwise."

Ellen nodded absently, her spirits considerably depressed at the moment. "One of my trifles? A fan perhaps, or my vinaigrette?"

"Aye, that's it!"

Ellen stood motionless, still regarding herself in the mirror. As she let her eyes travel over the costume that barely concealed her breasts and whose dampened fabric clung to her legs, she wailed, "Oh, Becky! I look just like a . . . a fashionable impure!"

Much to Ellen's surprise, the door snapped shut suddenly, and a feminine voice intruded. "You most certainly do. Ellen, what are you thinking? You cannot possibly mean to wear that gown. Why, I begin to think it is a very good thing I have come to London after all!"

Ellen caught sight of her sister's reflection in the mirror, and she stared at her, disbelieving. "Celeste! Why, whatever are you doing here?"

Ellen whirled around to face her sister and felt a surprising rush of emotion. It struck her suddenly how very alone and vulnerable she had been feeling, with only Becky as confidante, and a rather flighty one at that. And though Celeste was herself not entirely reliable, her mere presence was an immediate comfort to Ellen. She would have rushed to her sister and given her a huge hug, but Celeste's horrified expression stopped her.

For the longest moment, Celeste remained standing near Ellen's four-poster bed, a hand grasping one of the curved cherrywood posts in order to support herself, gaping at her elder sister. Her face grew quite pale, her eyes fixed upon the extreme décolleté of Ellen's gown, as she cried, "Ellen, your bosom!" She then released the bedpost, pressed her sealskin muff close to her heart, and with her blue eyes wide and unblinking, promptly crumpled to the floor.

"Celly! Celly! Oh, dear, she has fainted! Becky, pray bring my lavender water: it is on the bedstand—no, there, on the other side of the bed, and my vinaigrette. Oh, I forgot, I already placed it in the gold silk reticule! Please hurry!"

By the time Becky had finally retrieved both of these essential articles, Ellen had dropped to the floor beside her sister and was cradling Celeste's head upon her lap. "Poor dear," she said in a soothing tone, and began wafting the vinaigrette beneath Celeste's nose.

Celeste moaned slightly and coughed, trying to pushed the pungent smell away from her nose. Finally her eyes fluttered open. But Ellen's decision to hold her sister in such proximity to the very object that had caused her to faint was perhaps not the wisest choice.

Celeste caught sight of the offending muslin, or lack of it, squeezed her eyes shut, and moaned, "I shall faint again!"

"Breathe deeply, my dear," Ellen said. "I did not mean to give you such a shock!"

Celeste rolled her eyes, looking anywhere but at the

offending costume, and in a weak voice, said, "How very improper you've become, Ellen. I'd no idea!"

"Hush, dearest. Try not to think about it. I shall explain it all to you in a very few minutes. Only, do take several very deep, slow breaths. I am afraid you will go off again."

When Celeste was sitting comfortably in a chair by the window, and every now and again wafting her own vinaigrette beneath her nose, Ellen addressed her in a quiet voice. "But, dearest, why have you come? I have such pressing matters here in London, and I am afraid—"

Celeste lifted her hand, cutting her off. "Ellen, why must you bear everything yourself? After you were gone, I had a long conversation with Mrs. Ewshott, and perhaps you don't remember, but you left both Papa's will and his letter to you sitting on your desk in the library."

Ellen, who had been kneeling beside her sister and patting her hand, leaned back on her heels. "Oh! I completely forgot. I was so desperate, you see, to come to London as quickly as possible!" Her shoulders drooped slightly. "Then you know everything. Isn't it the most reprehensible will you have ever heard of?"

"Yes," Celeste said, her expression stormy as she pursed her lips together. "And isn't it just like Papa to force your hand in this manner! I am all out of patience with him, and if he hadn't perished in that wretched sailing accident, I would most certainly have given him a severe scold. And Bracknell! Why, even I know he possesses such gaming propensities as to equal Ambrose. What could Papa have been thinking?" She turned her head slightly, another expression of distaste suffusing her face as she glanced down at the décolleté of Ellen's gown. Closing her eyes again, she lifted the vinaigrette to her nose and again sniffed deeply. "But, Ellen, is that . . . that thing you are wearing quite necessary?"

Ellen rose to her feet. "I don't know. Becky seems to feel it is, and though I wish it were otherwise, I believe her reasoning to be sound. I have less than a month to win

Lord Bracknell, and how else am I to do it except by breaking one or two of society's strictures. I certainly don't want to, but I feel I must. How angry I am with our papa!" She stamped her foot lightly on the carpet of rose and lavender swirls, and with much frustration remembered the letter yet again: "spoiled manner of throwing fits." Oh, merciful heavens, how was she ever to win Lord Bracknell when her heart was so set against it?

Celeste nodded, her finely arched brows puckered. "And who am I to advise you when I . . . I actually eloped when I was fifteen." She was silent for a moment, snapping and unsnapping the lid of her vinaigrette in an absent-minded fashion. Finally she said, "Ambrose may be my husband, and though I should have some loyalty to him as . . . as a dutiful wife . . . I know what he is. He would ruin the estate in a year's time! I only hope Bracknell is not so very bad. But never mind that. Surely Mr. Ibthorpe could have papers drawn up to protect the property, or something of that nature. I do mean to help you all I can, and at the very least, I intend to become your chaperon. Why, with me along you may flirt with Bracknell as often as you please, and it will all be perfectly acceptable, for I am a matron." She spoke this last statement with the pleased air of a child, and Ellen laughed at her, grasping her hands and squeezing them gently.

"How glad I am that you have come to London. And perhaps we might even have a little fun, Celly, as we were used to do."

Celeste's blue eyes filled with tears suddenly. "I made a great mull of my life by marrying Ambrose, didn't I? And now Papa has ruined your life by insisting on your marriage to Bracknell. What a dreadful coil. But do let us try to have a little fun and gig; after all we have nearly four weeks before you must be leg-shackled to Lord Bracknell."

Ellen shook her head laughing ruefully. "Only you, dearest Celly, could make me want to laugh and cry in the very same moment."

* * *

When a commotion belowstairs announced the arrival of Bracknell and his two bosom bows, Ellen sent commands flying about the house for a suitable costume to be found in the attics for Celeste—one of Ellen's cast-off Elizabethan gowns, no doubt—for the gentlemen to be plied with sherry, and for Becky to revive Celeste's hair with her clever fingers. She only hoped their tardiness would in no way affect her ability to enchant Lord Bracknell, but Becky assured her a gentleman's interest could be piqued by such tricks as making him wait. In this Ellen was not convinced. Bracknell struck her as just the sort of man who would tire all too easily of such absurd feminine antics.

The gentlemen, however, were not aware of any particularly noxious passage of time since they were fully occupied with an event of great import.

Bracknell stared down at a fly scuttling along on a very fine occasional table of cherrywood, and shook his head. A candle, dripping profusely with runnels of wax and shooting little bursts of flame had obviously confused the day creature—the fly behaving as though night were still held at bay. Its progress was erratic, and Bracknell addressed the gentleman on his right. "The second lump of wax, not the first. Ten pounds."

The three men bent over the table, their heads nearly touching. Jeremy Andover heard the viscount's wager, nodded his head, and scribbled on a small sheet of paper, which, in addition to the critical bets of the moment, also bore several words grouped in rhyming pairs. He was a hopeful poet, very thin, with an interestingly pale complexion and soulful brown eyes. Turning to the third gentleman, he asked, "And you, Laurence?"

Laurence Chawton stroked his chin in a thoughtful fashion, a movement that never failed to amuse his friends. He had a brilliant mind, but it was so very much at odds with his round, freckled face that any curious affectations, such as rubbing the side of his nose or stroking his chin, as he just had, appeared absurd in the extreme. However, he had startling blue eyes, his most complimented feature, and an amiable temperament, which procured him a place at many a lady's table, where any number of greater men were denied. But in the true manner of a student of science, he had an eccentric habit of applying scientific principles, in a sometimes annoying fashion, to every aspect of his life. His current experiments involved the amount of wine he could consume in an evening without passing out. So, it was to no one's surprise when in answering Jeremy's question, he responded in his precise manner: "Judging by the propensity of the fly to move back and forth in a two-three pattern—two steps right, three steps left—our man shall certainly hit the first bit of wax in less than thirty seconds." And nodding wisely as though he had just laid down a profound law of physics that would have astonished even Newton, he finished with "Fifteen quid." In his hand he held a very fine watch, the scrolled silver case popped open, and his eyes moved very rapidly from the fly to the watch and back.

"You're both wrong," Jeremy said, his voice holding an edge of excitement. "He shall fly away without singeing his wings on this pillar of death. Ten quid."

Bracknell and Laurence stared at the poet, and in unison cried, "Pillar of death?"

Jeremy blushed slightly and mumbled, "Well, yes, perhaps it was a trifle overdone." And after clearing his throat turned his attention fully to the insect upon whose movements the outcome of the wager depended.

The room grew silent except for the sound of the door opening quietly and the butler entering with a stately tread. Mr. Binley, a short but powerfully built man who had served in the Warfield town house for more than thirty-five of his fifty years, wore a frown of extreme disapproval on his face as he waited patiently for the gentlemen to complete their present involvement. He carried a silver tray bearing three meagerly filled glasses of sherry. He did not wish to add to the great volume of spirits most gentlemen were wont to consume these days, particularly when these gentlemen—though he referred to them as such only through clenched teeth—were to escort Miss Warfield and

Mrs. Hazeley to that notorious, rackety pleasure haunt known as Vauxhall.

The frown deepened on his face as he regarded the backs of the gentlemen before him. He did not approve of Vauxhall, and he did not approve of masquerades. He did not approve of any of the strange doings that had been transpiring in the house since Miss Warfield returned from the country with that very improper female, Miss Lovedean, in tow. And he certainly did not think these rum coves should be squiring the young females of the house anywhere, especially to the debauched pleasure gardens. Had he been consulted upon the matter, he most assuredly would have sent the ladies to bed with warmed milk and turned the "gentlemen" away from the door before ever they lifted the brass knocker.

Two groans and a shout of triumph erupted suddenly from the gentlemen grouped about the cherrywood table, and Binley nearly lost control of the silver tray as he took a startled step backward.

Bracknell addressed his compatriots. "I shall expect payment forthwith. I haven't a guinea for this evening's entertainment."

Jeremy cried, "You've the devil's own luck, Hugh. Did you bring that fly along just to torment us?"

The men turned almost as one as they spied the servant, and each took a glass of sherry, regarding with considerable surprise the rather nipcheese portion each had been parceled out.

Binley announced in a dignified manner. "I beg to inform you Miss Warfield has been detained for a few minutes. She also wished me to inform you her sister, Mrs. Hazeley, will be joining the party."

"What?" Jeremy cried, choking on his sherry. And as the butler frowned on him severely, he felt compelled to explain, "I expect I was a little surprised. Yes, that's it! Just didn't know another female would be present." And he tugged at his shirtpoints hoping his face was not quite as red as it felt and then hurriedly drained what he soon found to be the smallest portion of sherry he had ever received in a lady's drawing room.

"As I was saying," Binley continued, scowling at each of the men in turn. "Miss Warfield hopes you will comport yourselves as gentlemen of breeding and manners."

"Does she?" Bracknell's lips twitched as he watched the disapproving expression on the retainer's face. He doubted Ellen would have instructed such a message to be delivered, and his hazel eyes twinkled in a mischievous fashion as he responded, "Please tell Miss Warfield we shan't tear the chandelier from the ceiling in a mad, drunken frenzy, if that is what has put her on the fret."

The butler took a menacing step toward Lord Bracknell. He didn't care if Gentleman Jackson had spoken highly of the viscount, praising his lordship's footwork, even admitting Bracknell had popped a few under his guard—no country work that! Binley too, was handy with his fives, and he knew he could spar with the best of 'em. He'd been in Warfield's service long before his lordship was out of short coats, and he stood as a father to Miss Ellen now, what with no men in the house to protect her. He did not hesitate to respond tartly, "And if I hear of any mischief, m'lord, you'll answer to me for it, which is how the master . . ." —he gestured to the portrait above the fireplace—"would have wanted it!"

He bowed ever so slightly, silver tray in hand, and as Bracknell watched him turn quietly away, he could not mistake the strong, muscular quality of the butler's short frame enhanced by the Warfield regalia, making it quite clear the man was fit to follow through on his words. He saw Vincent's training clearly enough. Only Warfield would hire such a fierce, fire-eating butler.

Bracknell turned to regard the the large portrait of Warfield. The style was very familiar: a Lawrence portrait of Vincent when he was younger and the fashion had been all brocades and lace, powder and wigs. The mischievous expression was Vincent to the life. What had the old man really planned to have happen in the next few weeks?

He sipped his sherry, glancing about the room, admiring

its quiet elegance and simplicity. Woods of varying shades reflected Vincent's influence, but he thought he saw Ellen's touch everywhere, in the delicate pastels, the beauty and fragrance of a variety of daffodils and roses set against the trailing green ivy, chairs upholstered in floral needlepoints, Sevres porcelain in several inconspicuous places.

Laurence stared at his empty glass in bewilderment and muttered that he couldn't consider a thimbleful of sherry to have the least impact upon his experiment. Setting his glass next to the sputtering candle, he turned to Bracknell, his expression thoughtful, and said, "And I still don't understand how you possibly knew which wax dripping that fly would gravitate toward. I was so certain it would be the one on the left. I watched the fly most carefully. I am completely mystified."

Bracknell was about to answer him with a teasing rejoinder, but the door opened and the ladies were suddenly with them. Somewhere in the recesses of his mind, he knew two women had entered the room, but he was only aware of a Grecian nymph who had stolen into the Warfield town house. Never had he seen Ellen's hair in such a delightful disarray—her golden curls in a burst of ringlets pulled very high on her head and permitted to fall to her shoulders. Adorning her white, creamy neck was a loop of emeralds; which served to draw his eyes—good God!—to her bosom. Now it was his turn to choke on his sherry as Jeremy had earlier, his gaze sliding over the rest of her costume, the golden bands about her waist, the delicate sandals strapped about her pretty feet. He thought he must be dreaming, and he realized in the past ten years never had he felt so strong an attraction to any female as he did in this moment to Ellen Warfield.

Ellen repressed a desire to hold a hand to her breast and silence the fierce beatings of her heart. She was frightened nearly out of her wits for fear Lord Bracknell, far from succumbing to her charms, would turn away from her in disgust. But as she watched him actually choke on his wine, Ellen knew instinctively her fears were ill-founded.

Then he gazed at her from head to toe, and something very nearly like admiration stole into his hazel eyes. Oh, how that very lascivious smile, which played at the corners of his mouth, brought a faint blush to her cheeks. She suddenly remembered meeting him in his town house and thought of his bare feet and the curly hairs on his toes. How very right Becky had been—he was a man like any other man. With these thoughts the terrible din of her heart, which had been pounding in her ears, began to subside. He was, she realized with a start, her ideal in so many ways. If only he were not a gamester!

Lawrence stepped forward and cried, "Miss Warfield!" He wasted no time in possessing himself of her fingers and kissing them lightly. "Truly a nymph," he cried. "How utterly charming, and so strictly in the Greek mode, a very fine precision of imitation. I congratulate you. You do remember me, I trust? We met once at the opera two years ago. *Le Nozze di Figaro*, I think."

Ellen breathed a sigh of relief, for their meeting came back to her suddenly, and she said, "It has been a long time, but I do remember you, Mr. Chawton. And I seem to recall you were very much engrossed of the moment in studying the theories of some unknown genius of the day by the name of—oh, dear, I can't quite remember, but I think it was something like Bolton, wasn't it?"

Laurence beamed. Never in his entire career had a female, particularly after so long a period of time, actually recalled a subject of his conversation. In a worshipful manner, he bowed to her slightly and replied, "Dalton—and his most fascinating concept of the atom."

"I remember being quite intrigued by the ideas you presented, and I should like to hear more of them. But won't you permit me to make you known to my sister, Mrs. Hazeley."

As he greeted Celeste, Ellen realized the other young man, who must have been Jeremy Andover, had already made her sister's acquaintance. A very small frown puckered her brow. Did they know each other? Ellen was struck with how very soft Jeremy's large brown eyes were as he gazed at Celeste, who in turn stared at the carpet, a faint smile on her lips.

Whatever the case, Laurence Chawton did not care for anyone stealing a march on him, and as he greeted Celeste, he frowned severely at Jeremy. But the poet seemed intent upon cutting Laurence out and sidled rather close to Celeste, admiring her costume, demanding to know if the white starched ruff about her neck was in the least troublesome and whether or not the Virgin Queen was one of her favorite personages from her schoolroom history lessons. Laurence, whose interest in history was nearly as great as his passion for the scientific realm, immediately interrupted with his own opinions. It was great irony, Ellen thought as she watched them vying for Celeste's attention, that these men were present for the strict purpose of making Bracknell jealous. Well, that had been Becky's idea, and she had never cared for it in the least anyway! In any case, their evident interest in Celeste had an unlooked-for benefit, since it afforded Bracknell the opportunity of drawing Ellen aside.

After placing a lingering kiss upon her gloved fingers, he led her to the fireplace for the ostensible purpose of finding out when the portrait of her papa had been painted.

When he asked to know the year of the actual sitting, Ellen replied, "I don't know precisely. I was only a little girl at the time, perhaps four or five. But it was all very exciting. Have you had your own portrait drawn?"

He shook his head, glancing down at her, at her fine, green eyes, wide with innocence and even a sincerity he found difficult to credit. "Perhaps in a few years, I might commission a portrait for the gallery at Three Elms." He was thoughtful for a time, turning to regard her profile as she gazed at her father's portrait, her expression a trifle sad. He felt a sudden and pressing need to expose her for what he believed her to be. In a low voice, he said, "You've quite bowled me over, you know. And such a wicked costume! However, might I suggest a little more subtlety in your efforts? Even I could see you mean to enchant Mr. Chawton in particular this evening—that nonsense of professing an interest in his conversation. Doing it a trifle too brown, Miss Warfield!"

The intense fear Ellen had experienced upon entering the drawing room had long since dissipated, so when he spoke in such an unkind fashion to her, as though her need to acquire a husband were accompanied by a harsh, unfeeling attitude toward others, she did not hesitate to respond hotly, "I resent your implications, Lord Bracknell. You know full well I must be married in a month's time, but I do not hesitate to tell you I spoke sincerely with your friend, without any reprehensible motive in mind, such as you suggest. I am not myself a student of science—I will not be so hypocritical to pretend as much—but I certainly found Mr. Chawton's ideas of merit. Do you doubt my character?"

"I wouldn't dare!" he responded, placing a hand at his heart, feigning shock. "But, given the circumstances, what else am I to think?"

Ellen shifted her gaze back to her father's portrait and did not know which face she detested more of the moment—her papa's for placing her in this wretched predicament, or Bracknell's for making it clear how little he esteemed her. She continued slowly, "I am in a very difficult situation, my lord. You know that . . ."—she turned to face him again, her anger returning in full measure as she finished,—"but that does not mean I must set aside my own principles of conduct in order to accomplish this wretched task."

He smiled in a perfectly infuriating manner as he responded, "You are telling whiskers, Miss Warfield, for how do you explain your costume this evening? Even I am aware no young lady of 'conduct,' to use your own words, would wear such a gown."

Ellen could have scratched his face for his superior expression as he smiled at her. But with hands clenched, she held herself in the strictest control, and responded in a coolly. "But I have been informed, my lord rake, by an extremely reliable source, that the only way I could possibly hope to engage the attention of a man quickly was to appeal to his physical senses rather than to his mind. You yourself choked quite thoroughly over your wine; do you deny that?"

He regarded the martial light in her eyes and felt the tip of an imaginary sword just touching his ribs. "A hit," he responded softly, a chuckle sounding deeply within his chest. "I admit you are right in this. We are weak creatures and will always be affected strongly by a pretty . . . " —he let his gaze fall to her bosom and finished with a smile—"costume. But where did you acquire such worldly knowledge, I wonder?"

Ellen was so surprised at his reaction, she couldn't respond for a moment. All his arrogance seemed to fall away when he laughed, and she saw a glimpse of the man, who, heaven help her, she was beginning to admire. Which of the puppies that usually romped about the skirts of the golden heiress would have matched her steel as he had? Finally she said, "I refuse to betray any of my secrets to you lest you fault me for some other supposed character defect."

He regarded her intently. Never in a thousand years would he have believed this female capable of engaging him in a battle of wits. Yet he should not have been surprised, because she was Vincent's daughter. This thought had an unfortunate effect, for it reminded him suddenly that he had a somewhat nefarious scheme of his own to implement—acquiring a fan, a kerchief, and a snuffbox from Ellen. And if he continued to set up her back, just how likely was it she would happily relinquish anything to him, let alone several quite personal articles?

Ellen lifted her brow, unable to comprehend the oddly assorted expressions traveling across his countenance. In an incredulous voice, she cried, "Have I actually silenced you?"

He laughed again, and was prepared to continue this most intriguing duel with her when Laurie approached them. "I vow, between you and Jeremy, I've been thoroughly cut out!"

Ellen, aware that the odd number of the party could prove quite uncomfortable to one of the gentlemen, immediately turned to Mr. Chawton saying Bracknell had been boring her anyway and asking him to please tell her more about Mr. Dalton's theories.

Bracknell regarded his friend with no small degree of amusement as Laurie stood very near to Ellen, his gaze drifting frequently to the emeralds and beyond. He could not help but wonder if his friend was reducing Ellen's figure to a mathematical sequence and was certain of it when, as they all moved downstairs and out onto the flagways, Laurence held him back a trifle, and whispered, "By god, I think every inch of her near to perfection. Even Harriette Wilson hasn't so fine a . . . a figure, and have you noticed her ankles?" Both men gazed at Ellen as she mounted the steps of Bracknell's town coach. Laurence sighed. "Neatly turned. Neatly turned!"

Bracknell surveyed the shapely feet encased in gold sandals, thinking he should like to nibble on her toes, then chided himself. He had no intention of falling prey to Miss Warfield's schemes, which he felt certain fully included him. Did she expect him to succumb to her wiles and to offer for her pretty face? How little she understood him. He had had too many beautiful girls set their caps for him not to know when a female was trying to fix her interest with him. But that did not mean he could not amuse himself. She was, after all, a dazzling creature.

An enchanting smile adorned Ellen's visage as she paused at the top of the carriage steps and turned back to face Bracknell, her skirts raised slightly. A sudden evening breeze drew back her shimmering domino in a billow of gold satin, the dampened muslin of her skirts exposing not only the ankles Laurence had admired with slavish adoration, but the outline of exquisitely shaped legs.

Bracknell could have sworn Vincent was with him in that moment, touching him on the shoulder, his hearty laughter rolling suddenly through Berkeley Square.

Chapter Six

ELLEN HELD HER gold silk mask, embroidered with an elegant Grecian motif, tightly in her hands. A sick feeling of anxiety had settled in the pit of her stomach, and her greatest fear of the moment was that someone at Vauxhall might recognize her. And what a grievous scandal would ensue, her reputation ruined forever, were she to be seen in so improper a costume. She could only hope if she tied her mask on with several knots, no one, particularly Lord Bracknell, would be able to remove it. Not for one moment was she unaware of her costume's scandalous quality, nor how often Bracknell regarded her gown, in a most discomfiting fashion, with an odd fire glinting in his hazel eyes.

As the coach rumbled through Berkeley Square Ellen became acutely aware that Jeremy's attention was fixed upon Celeste in a rather alarming manner. He was seated across from her sister and was staring at her in a fashion that would have thrown even the most brazen of females into a state of confusion.

Celeste was clearly uncomfortable with Jeremy's scrutiny, for she sat nervously pulling at the strings of her white beaded reticule and more often than not kept her gaze firmly fixed upon whatever brick buildings happened to be passing by the window. She even jumped when Bracknell asked her if she enjoyed reading poetry. Mumbling an incomprehensible answer, Celeste again turned to regard the scenery, commenting on the ever-present fog clinging drearily to the gaslights along Oxford Street.

Ellen was mystified by her sister's nervousness, for in general Celeste was fond of all manners of dalliance, and more particularly of the attention of handsome, young gentlemen. And Jeremy Andover was quite handsome, she thought, his dark brown hair swept in a wild yet attractive disarray, his large, brown eyes fixed broodingly upon Celeste. A man born to wrestle with the muse, certainly, and even now he was speaking to Celeste of a sonnet that had held him in thrall for several weeks—something about a celestial goddess.

Silence reigned within the coach for several minutes after Jeremy's description of his latest poem. Finally he addressed the object of his extreme interest, "Haven't I met you before, Mrs. Hazeley? Perhaps last year or the year before at Almack's?"

Celeste shifted in her seat as she adjusted her red velvet skirts, her blue eyes darting from Jeremy to Bracknell and back again. In a disjointed manner, she responded, "Yes, that is, no! At least, I'm not certain, for I have been positively buried in Hampshire these past several years, and I have not been to London in at least three."

"Then you have missed a great deal. I hope you will enjoy the evening's masquerade," Jeremy said.

If Ellen didn't know better, she would have thought Jeremy was in some manner teasing her sister. Celeste, however, seemed to relax at his words and pulled gently at the ruff of her gown. "I think I shall, Mr. Andover. Indeed, I do." Lifting her chin, she added, "That is, if you would please stop staring at me as though you've seen a specter, Mr. Andover. You have quite unnerved me."

He seemed almost taunting as he responded, "But you are very beautiful, and I have a sudden inspiration to write a poem in your honor. Would you permit me to do so, Mrs. Hazeley?"

These words only caused Celeste to become flustered all over again and she sputtered, "Why, of all the nonsense—that is, you must do as pleases you, I am sure!"

* * *

The lilting rhythms of a waltz greeted Ellen as she descended the steps of the town coach, her gold silk reticule dangling from her wrist. She felt suddenly lighthearted at the vision of Vauxhall, a thousand lanterns shimmering on the Thames, and at the riotous sound of hundreds of merrymakers enjoying the orchestra, the dancing, and, undoubtedly, the shadowed walkways, where a dozen kisses could be exchanged. Vauxhall. She sighed with pleasure, for she had always enjoyed the gardens.

Ellen pulled her fur-lined domino closely about the scandalous costume, certainly for protection against the cool night air but very much as well to ward off the leering stares of several half-foxed gentlemen who lined the entrance and ogled every female who walked by wearing silks or muslins. Ellen again touched her mask, which covered nearly half her face, and let out a breath of air she did not even realize she was holding. No one could possibly recognize her now. Because she was in Lord Bracknell's company, assuredly she would be set down as his latest mistress and ignored completely by members of the beau monde, she thought with a rueful smile.

Laurence entered the hall before Ellen and Bracknell, and laughed outright at the vision before him. Turning around with a jeering expression on his face, he whispered, "What is the significance of this pair? A cow escorting the queen of the nile? I daresay the Bard could have made something of this? What do you think, Jeremy?"

Jeremy had just released Celeste's hand, although it had been several minutes since he had helped her descend the coach. After spying the object of Laurie's amusement, he answered quietly, "Oh, yes, indeed. Shakespeare most certainly would have made an entire first act of it."

Ellen found the object of the gentlemen's attention, and she, too, smiled, for the newly arrived masqueraders were an interesting combination. But when the man sporting the bovine confection threw his cumbersome head back and laughed, Ellen nearly fainted. His laughter sounded just like her papa's, and her heart constricted painfully in her breast, sudden tears burning her eyes. In the past several months since her father's death, she had often been afflicted in just this manner when something quite insignificant, in this case an absurd brown and white cow, put her forcibly in mind of the terrible loss she had suffered. How much she missed her papa.

She turned to face her sister, whose stricken gaze was also fixed upon the cow. Ellen placed a hand on the soft velvet sleeve of Celeste's gown and whispered, "Celly, did you hear that? Am I imagining something?"

Celeste's face had grown very pale, and for a moment Ellen thought she might faint. "It was Papa's voice," she answered. And they both stared very hard at Cleopatra and the cow as they disappeared into the crowd. Taking a deep breath, attempting to maintain her composure, Celeste tried for a lighter tone, "He would even have worn such a costume. Only I think he would have dressed as a bull rather than as a tame heifer."

Ellen slipped her arm about her sister's waist and gave her a squeeze. "Yes, at the very least a bull, with fierce horns!" And the ladies exchanged a look of sympathy along with a nod, which meant they would set aside the hurt of the moment and tend rather to the business at hand.

This was fortunate, for the gentlemen had suddenly become quite intrigued by several females of dubious occupation, gowned in Roman costumes so short as to reveal a large portion of their legs. This would not do, and Ellen cleared her throat several times until the men were fully restored to their duties.

As they made their progression to their box, Ellen delighted in looking at all the costumes, from quite scandalous females dressed as butterflies to knights bearing coats of mail, to—good heavens—Cleopatra and the cow again, who were sitting in the box next to their own. And, oh, dear, the Egyptian queen was ogling Lord Bracknell. But then, Ellen could scarcely blame her. The viscount, even with his identity concealed behind his mask, still had a commanding presence.

Ellen whispered to him, "You have conquered yet another heart, my lord rake!"

He seemed a little startled, and Ellen laughed at him. "Do but look, though as unobtrusively as possible. Our Cleopatra has taken a fancy to you."

Lord Bracknell refused to oblige Ellen by turning to stare at the sultry queen, and instead seated her with a shake of his head. "How very improper were I to begin flirting with another female."

He was standing over Ellen, his hands on the back of her chair, and she looked up at him and retorted archly, "Why, Lord Bracknell, what a bouncer. For I did not have the least impression you were flirting with *any* female of the moment. How am I to take this? To whom were you referring? For I know very well the moment I should attempt to flirt with you, I would be rebuked for *conduct* unbecoming a lady of quality."

The amused glint in his eye returned in full measure as he met her gaze. "I was hoping we would return to our earlier conversation." He remembered also that he ought to treat Ellen with a little more kindness since she possessed three articles he needed desperately, and he added, "I wish to apologize for my incivilities. I behaved in a most ungentlemanly manner."

Ellen thought this a rather sudden shift for Lord Bracknell, but she accepted his gracious apology quite readily and replied, "Yes, quite unchivalrous, particularly when you promised to flirt with me, if you remember?"

He leaned close to her ear and startled her by whispering, "How very well I recall the promise I made to you. But more significantly the very improper manner in which you kissed me."

Ellen was shocked, first that he would mention the matter at all, and then because he had the audacity to accuse her of being the perpetrator. She pressed a hand against her bosom and cried in an incredulous voice, "I?"

He pulled a chair forward for Celeste, who was regarding this interchange with great interest, her blue eyes wide, and seated her carefully. After Celeste thanked him, he turned to Ellen, and with a devilish smile on his lips, prompted her, "Yes? What were you going to say?"

Ellen knew he had placed her in an impossible position, for she could scarcely refute his taunting remark without revealing to all of them that she had actually permitted Lord Bracknell to kiss her. Glancing at him in a defiant manner, her chin high, her green eyes sparkling, she cried, "You are an unconscionable rogue!"

The gentlemen seated themselves, and Laurence exclaimed, "Eh, what's this? Has Miss Warfield discovered the truth already? Hugh, you are destined to fail in your attempts to break her heart! I recommend you leave her entirely to me."

Ellen went down the first dance, a waltz, with Laurence, the second, a tame country dance, with Lord Bracknell, and the quadrille with Jeremy. Laurence's movements were what she had come to expect of him—a precision of steps wholly lacking in either style or sensibility—and the waltz they shared seemed rather flat to her. Jeremy, on the other hand, performed his part in the quadrille in the opposite fashion, for he missed any number of the intricate steps, and included a great flourishing of his arms, completely unnecessary to the precise nature of the dance. She thought if she could arrange it, she would insist upon dancing any future quadrilles with the scientist and extract from the poet a promise that he would waltz with her. As for Lord Bracknell, throughout the country dance they shared he teased her so thoroughly regarding how improper she had become that she missed many of her steps and quit the dance floor with her cheeks flushed a dull red. Very typically, the rogue enjoyed her discomfiture.

Between dances, Ellen sipped her champagne, and often found her gaze drawn to their near-neighbors. Perhaps it was merely the proximity of the boxes, but she found more often than not, when she glanced in their direction, either Cleopatra or the awkward cow had their heads turned toward Lord Bracknell's box. At one point Ellen again heard a rumble of laughter that so completely put her in mind of her father as to cause a second little shot of pain to course through her heart.

Celeste seemed inclined to converse primarily with Jeremy, and after an hour or so, was completely at ease with the poet, her face and gestures animated, her giggles quite frequent. Jeremy, as it happened, had provided precisely what her sister needed—an adoring expression on his handsome face as he stared at her, with a promise to compose a dozen verses in her honor before the moon crested again upon the night skies. Celeste called him absurd, slapped his arm with her mother-of-pearl fan, and begged him to continue, which he did quite readily.

A fine supper followed another country dance, and a fifth bottle of champagne was brought to the table. Ellen didn't know precisely when she had started keeping count of the bottles, but she thought it was when Laurence tried to place his elbow on the table, missed, and landed his cheek squarely into his peas and onions. As the bottle was poured round, Ellen turned her gaze to Laurence, her brows raised, her green eyes wide with wonder, as he very slowly reached for his glass and promptly knocked it over.

Ellen turned her astonished gaze to Bracknell, who said, "You must ask him about his latest scientific endeavor."

Ellen laughed outright, unable to imagine what the viscount could possibly mean, then turned to Laurence and begged to know precisely what interesting work he was currently engaged in.

Laurie regarded Ellen with a silly smile, his blue eyes nearly crossed, appearing even younger than usual as he sputtered, "I am in the process of determining my capacity for wine. Any sort of wine—champagne, port, sherry—although I must inform you I do not consider the sherry your rather clutch-fisted butler poured out for us of the least significance." He nodded quite sloppily to Ellen and added, "I hope I don't offend you by saying so."

Ellen tilted her head slightly, unable to keep from smiling at Laurence as she responded, "Oh, dear. I daresay Binley was a trifle disapproving of our excursion this evening, for whenever he wishes to discourage any of my visitors, he fills the glasses but a quarter full. I do apologize."

Laurence nodded in an approving manner to Ellen and

reached over to pat her shoulder. "Wasn't your fault at all." By now his lids were drooping ominously. He patted his coat pockets and finally said, "I can't seem to locate my pencil. I must make a notation of the time, for I seem . . ." —he paused, his eyes rolling about in his head—"that is, I have a very queer feeling . . ." His eyes disappeared entirely, his shoulders slumped forward and—thanks to Jeremy's quick action, for he removed a plate, a fork, and a champagne glass—barely escaped injury as he collapsed unconscious upon the table.

Ellen jumped back in her seat, and Lord Bracknell addressed the poet. "Have you a pencil, Jeremy? You know what he will be in the morning if one of us has not recorded the time. He will badger us to return to Vauxhall on the morrow and attempt to reconstruct the evening entirely!"

Jeremy shook his head, and Lord Bracknell supplicated the ladies for a writing implement. Ellen immediately drew open her reticule and removed her vinaigrette, the kerchief her papa had given her, and a small silver comb. She then searched the bottom of the gold silk confection, where ordinarily any number of miscellaneous articles might assemble, but no pencil proved to have the least interest in consorting with a pair of tiny peacock embroidery scissors, a loop of white thread, and a small cylinder of bone containing several steel needles. "I haven't anything here that would suit your purposes," she said with a smile, and she began returning the articles to her reticule.

Celeste also responded that she did not have a pencil, and Lord Bracknell was about to suggest they all take mental note of the time in order to corroborate the hour for Laurence's experiment, when his gaze happened to fall upon Ellen's gold-embroidered kerchief just as she was putting it away. Good god, he had almost forgotten his mission, and there before him, now safely tucked within Ellen's reticule, was the first prize. His heart immediately began pounding. How many times over the years had these moments occurred when he had been working on a project with Vincent? It was always the same for him—an incredible heightening of his senses, his heart rushing in his ears. How the devil was he to get the object from Ellen? Or more to the point, how was he to accomplish the task without in some manner leading her to believe he was trying to fix his interest with her?

He removed his gold watch from his waistcoat pocket and checked the time. "I have nearly midnight. I shall inform Laurence tomorrow, and you may all stand as witnesses."

Celeste and Jeremy both nodded in agreement, the former covering her mouth with her hand suddenly, to repress the laughter threatening to overcome her as she viewed Laurie's freckled face resting upon the table.

Ellen, on the other hand, felt suddenly uncomfortable. She had seen something she did not understand, an enigmatic expression on Lord Bracknell's face as he eyed the kerchief. Slowly pulling the strings of her gold reticule, Ellen suddenly remembered what Becky had told her to do—to try and entrust one of her trifles into Lord Bracknell's care. Well, perhaps Becky had used the phrase "to saddle him with a personal article," but the result would be the same—he would then have in his possession a continual reminder of her.

Bracknell had seemed impressed for some reason by the kerchief, so it seemed now quite a logical thing for Ellen to attempt to give it to him. Why, then, did she feel so uneasy about it, except when Lord Bracknell had fixed his gaze upon the kerchief, a very odd expression—nothing, surely!—had settled upon his face, and his eyes for the briefest second had brightened in a curious manner. She was disturbed, but she didn't know why.

As she settled her reticule upon her lap, Ellen chided herself for being such a ninnyhammer. Undoubtedly Bracknell thought the handkerchief a trifle unusual, which it was, for it had a very intricate pattern of embroidery about the edges. And with that thought, she returned her attention to the conversation at hand, which, she discovered, involved a matter of great amusement—the fireworks display.

The gentlemen had decided Laurence was perfectly comfortable where he was. After Lord Bracknell summoned their waiter and politely asked him to see their friend was attended to, and after he had assured himself of the waiter's service by pressing a guinea into his hand, the small party joined the crowds now making a noisy and sometimes bawdy progress toward the display.

Ellen and Celeste clapped their hands in delight at every explosion and burst of color that lit the skies above the gardens. The cool air was soon filled with the acrid smell of flash-power, but they didn't care. Spring in London could be an enchanting time, and every spark that shimmered for a moment against the black, starlit sky, was one that removed Ellen for just a moment from her every difficulty.

And when the display was over, some of the magic remained with her as she turned up the path. Lord Bracknell held her elbow securely, for the crowds had begun pushing and jostling—it seemed they all desired posthaste to return to their boxes, to their champagne, to flirting, and to dancing. Ellen looked for Celeste but could not find her.

"What an unruly lot!" Bracknell cried, as two butterflies pushed past him toward the opposite direction.

Ellen laughed, feeling exhilarated by the evening's events, and as the path in front of them cleared, and the strains of a heavenly waltz met her ears, she looked up at the viscount and cried, "If we were to run, which is most improper, I know, we could possibly be the very first couple to begin the waltz!"

Lord Bracknell could not resist the excitement in Ellen's voice, nor the glitter in her eyes, and he quickly took her by the arm and set them both off at a run. Ellen laughed the entire way, and once they arrived, she slipped easily into his arms, as though she had done so a hundred times, and they began whirling about the floor.

Jeremy did not care in the least what his friends thought, or even what Miss Warfield thought. He had only one desire, and did not hesitate, once the fireworks ended, to guide Celeste toward a darkened path, silencing her protests by tucking her hand about his arm and saying "Hush, my love. Don't you see providence has brought us together. I could scarcely believe you were to join us this evening, and when your sister's butler actually said 'Mrs. Hazeley,' I nearly fell over! Olympus has smiled upon us, my darling. We are bound through eternity by every sacred grove that ever held an oracle." And he gestured about him.

Celeste giggled. "But, Jeremy, I should hardly call the gardens at Vauxhall a sacred grove! Quite the contrary, I should think," she added, feeling very bold since they were at that moment passing by a couple locked in a tight embrace.

Suddenly, as the reality of the nearness of her beloved poet burst upon her, she cried, "Oh, Jeremy, my dearest love! I am in the midst of a beautiful dream. Are you really beside me? Are we together at last?" She watched his face intently, afraid if she averted her gaze for even a moment, he might disappear.

Jeremy looked down into her deep blue eyes and felt yet again an urgency that always assailed him when he was with her. He wanted to steal her away, to call upon Pegasus to transport them to a better world, where their love might find expression. But no winged horse answered his summons, and being of a somewhat practical turn of mind regardless of his poetic leanings, he hurried her down a path toward the River Thames, the shadows deepening beneath the bare scattering of lamps strung throughout the trees.

When there was no one in sight, and shadows covered them, he stopped abruptly. "My beloved," he said, then pulled her roughly into his arms and kissed her. But it was hardly the most satisfactory experience, for the ruff of Celeste's gown caught his chin, and though he tried to press the ruff down, it was painfully starched. Finally he drew back from her, his eyes watering. "Cursed thing!" he cried, using both his hands to try to flatten it against her shoulders. But the thick, fluted collar was quite incorrigible, and he had to content himself with kissing her and holding the ruff down at the same time.

This only made Celeste giggle, which in turn made Jeremy surprisingly content. "How happy I am to see you smiling," he said. "But, my dear, it is the hour for deciding our future. I am grown desperate, especially being with you tonight. My darling, elope with me. We can be at my estate in Scotland in but a few days. We'll collect Marcus and Julian . . . " He broke off at the sad expression on her face and stepped back from her slightly. Letting his hands slide down the red velvet covering her arms, he caressed her gently, then, taking her chin in his hand, he asked, "What is it, my pet?"

Celeste met his gaze, her eyes bright with tears, and in a quiet voice, she said, "But I am married, Jeremy. I have a husband, and what of my sons, and what of Ellen? How can I bring such a scandal down about their ears? Don't you see . . . " —she touched his cheek with her gloved hand—"I already hurt my family so very much when I eloped with Ambrose seven years ago. How could I possibly do it again?"

His expression was infinitely tender as he smiled down at her. "But you would not be eloping with Ambrose again, my dear."

She tugged a wavy brown lock of his hair and chided him, "Oh, don't be so absurd; you will make me cry. You know very well I was not referring to him." And she sniffed loudly.

Jeremy drew her into an embrace, cradling her head on his shoulder, and held her very close. And though this time the errant ruff bit into his ear, he paid it no heed, but held her more tightly still. "We shall find a way, my love. I know we shall. I love you too much to let this be the end of the matter."

And though he tried to kiss her again, the business was so awkward that he told her to burn the ruff when she got home—and certainly never to wear one again in his presence. Celeste in turn placed a tender kiss upon his cheek, and they turned to head back up the path, where the strains of a waltz could be heard through the trees.

* * *

Perhaps it was the champagne, Ellen thought, or maybe the way the lanterns cast mesmerizing shadows upon Lord Bracknell's face, but whatever the cause, she felt dizzy. They whirled and swayed, back and forth, around and around to the waltz, her gold cape and Lord Bracknell's black domino billowing out behind them both. She felt lighthearted and so very much alive. Surely it was because of the waltz, or the champagne, she thought, but in the secret place of her heart, she knew it was solely because of the man who led her easily about the floor. He had succeeded in charming her, and she felt frightened suddenly of his power to have done so. Would that the waltz might end, that she could return safely to their box and to Celeste's protective presence.

But when the waltz ended, instead of returning her to her sister, Lord Bracknell slipped an arm about Ellen's waist and guided her quickly to the shadowed pathways of the gardens. In a whisper, as he swept her along, he teased her. "I am sorry for it, Miss Warfield, but you are in the company of a rake—as you so politely informed me not two days ago—and I daresay I now have a certain debauched reputation to maintain. You must walk the shadows with me. At least for a little while until your chaperon returns."

Ellen felt her cheeks burn as they moved deep into the gardens. Oh, dear, she thought. Would he try to kiss her again? And then a far worse thought entered her mind—what if he did not try at all? It struck Ellen, with all the force of hidden desires suddenly uncovered, that she wanted nothing more than to be held in the circle of his arms again and to be kissed, quite thoroughly, just as he had done before. Her heart began beating rather wildly at these thoughts. But why did she wish for his embraces? No other gentleman of her acquaintance had ever prompted such desires, only Bracknell, a notorious gamester and rake, who had stolen dozens of innocent hearts, torn them asunder, and scattered them all about Mayfair for years on end. She despised him.

Yet there was so much about him that truly pleased her.

His noble carriage, for one thing, and the manner in which he was always watching everything about him—he was very alive to his world. And another thing—he refused to dance about her skirts, as so many younger gentlemen did, composing ridiculous love billets to her and waiting for hours outside her door in hopes of catching a mere glimpse of her. The shadows grew deeper and deeper as did the terrible ambivalence she felt toward the man next to her. Why must he be a gamester—anything but that! Why could he not have possessed lesser faults, such as using an inferior blacking on his boots or pomading his hair, as Ambrose did? Why must he be a gamester?

She glanced up at him again, wishing she could cast a magical potion upon his head and erase his predilection for dice and cards, and then her life might be perfect. He turned at that moment and smiled down at her, and her heart again fluttered in her breast. Faith, but he was an overpowering creature, even with part of his face concealed behind a mask. On an impulse she let his arm go and reached to pull the strings of his mask. He laughed as the black silk mask fell away, and he caught it lightly, saying, "Then I insist upon removing yours."

"Oh, but you can't," she cried, her green eyes twinkling. "For I have tied it in knots."

He narrowed his eyes at her and retorted, "I consider that a challenge, Miss Warfield." And he spun her around and attacked the little knots. He cursed several times in the process of attempting to untie the ribbons, and once or twice he pulled so hard that Ellen felt it necessary to rebuke his clumsiness. But after he removed his gloves, and drew her near to a lantern where he might better see the offending knots, he soon had the task complete, lifting the mask gently from her face.

He caught his breath as he looked down at her. How did it happen, he wondered, that he had forgotten of the moment how very beautiful she was. Not that the scandalous gown had kept his interest elsewhere—not much! She was an exquisite creature, and the most ignoble thought crossed his mind—he should have enjoyed making her his mistress, were she not a gently nurtured female. How kissable she appeared! For the past two hours at least, he had found it difficult to keep from just reaching out and touching her hair, or the silky skin on her arms when her cape fell back a trifle. Many times he had found it necessary to banish the thought of what it would feel like to kiss her throat, right above the emeralds.

But she was here now, and the feelings he had been suppressing all evening rushed in on him. "Damn," he cried, slipping an arm about her waist, feeling the thin muslin of her gown. But he did not kiss her right away. Instead he cradled her head gently for a moment, regarding her steadily, "I know I should not be doing this, but you are partly to blame, Miss Warfield. You should never have worn this costume, at least not without expecting one or two dastardly consequences."

"The thought had crossed my mind," Ellen replied in a whisper, remembering how distressed she had been earlier in the evening.

He breathed lightly upon her cheek, kissing her several times and reveling in the softness of her skin. He let his lips play gently upon hers, marveling at how delicate they felt beneath his own.

Ellen could scarcely endure these soft, teasing motions for she longed desperately to have him kiss her in earnest. When she thought she could bear it no longer, she cried, "Bracknell, pray, cease tormenting me!" But he was not so kind as to oblige her, and she felt his mouth hover barely upon her own until she could scarcely breathe, and only then did he kiss her.

Somewhere in her mind Ellen knew permitting a gentleman to kiss her before ever she was engaged was improper in the extreme. But what was she to do? His lips had completely charmed her. Leaning into him fully, Ellen reached up to touch the hair at the back of his neck. This seemed to please him, for he kissed her harder still.

Lord Bracknell wondered what the devil he was doing trifling with Ellen's sensibilities so completely. He released her, intending to return her to their box. But when he looked into her glittering green eyes, cloaked with desire, he was suddenly overwhelmed by the need to hold her again, which he did, embracing her fiercely, devouring her mouth in a most ungentlemanly fashion and finding at the moment he wished the evening would never end.

On another path Cleopatra spoke in a soothing voice to her bovine companion. "There, there, he's done naught but what you'd do in the same situation. And he's only kissing her, or did you think he'd behave the gentleman?"

"It's that devilish gown she's sporting. How could you have let her wear such a confounded—"

"Oh, hush. She's havin' a bit of fun is all!" And Cleopatra took the cow forcefully by the arm and pulled him down another path. "And just remember, he's under the strictest instructions to break her heart, in case you be forgetting that one particular inspiration of yours!"

The cow grumbled as he trudged beside the Egyptian queen, his thick costume hanging lumpily about his ankles. "I should've left you in that cursed theater in Tunbridge Wells where I found you!"

But Cleopatra was not daunted in the least and responded happily, "I've told you so often and often!"

Ellen did not realize at what point she grew uncomfortable with the impropriety of her actions, but she thought it was when one of Lord Bracknell's hands drifted over her hip. Good gracious, how very bad she had become!

Pulling away from him suddenly, Ellen pressed her hands to her cheeks, her eyes filling with tears, and cried, "Oh, my! Oh, dear, what am I doing?" She turned away from the viscount, fully intending to run back to their box, to the lights, to the safety of Celeste's side, but he caught her arm.

In a kind voice, he said, "Gently, Miss Warfield. Wait! Your mask." He was concerned, suddenly, for her reputation. Were she to be recognized in that gown, he knew quite well she would be shunned from polite society. His own conscience smote him terribly, and he said, "I do most sincerely apologize."

Ellen took several deep breaths, and blinked back her tears. With her gaze fixed on the ground, she permitted him to retie the mask. When he had completed this task, she turned to face him and in a subdued manner, said, "You have nothing to apologize for, my lord. I would be a hypocrite to place the blame upon you. The truth is, I wanted you to kiss me, but . . . but it is so very wrong!"

He looked down at her, which was most certainly a mistake, for it only increased his desire to kiss her again. "Indeed, very wrong."

And as he regarded her, he remembered suddenly that he had a matter of business to attend to. Damme, he did not wish to take advantage of the situation, but what else could he do, particularly when he knew the kerchief he had been instructed to acquire was in Ellen's reticule. Taking her by the arm, he began guiding her up the path, and said, "I admire you greatly, Miss Warfield, and I promise you I shall not importune you again. But I wonder if you might humor me in something quite frivolous?" He paused, feeling like a dog in the manger, but he knew his duty.

Ellen responded softly, "I should be happy to oblige you, if it is within my power."

He said, "Would you consider parting with your kerchief that I might have a token of our masquerade at Vauxhall?"

In the early hours of the morning, when the sounds of Lord Bracknell's town coach had long since disappeared from Berkeley Square, and Ellen's hair had been wrapped in curl papers and tucked beneath a mobcap, she reviewed the evening's events with Becky. Once in bed, she related with great animation everything that had occurred, including a lively recital about their neighbors—the Queen of the Nile and the cow. This portion Becky seemed to enjoy more than any other, for she laughed heartily at the very thought of such an odd pair, and then begged Ellen to continue. Ellen did so, quite happily, and with a strong sense that she had made considerable progress in her schemes. But when she described just how she had relinquished her kerchief to the viscount, who in turn had pressed her hand in a most pleasing manner, she fell silent, her brow puckered.

"What is it, miss? You look sick-like all of a sudden, and from what I've heard, why, you should be pleased with this night's work!" Becky pulled the rose-flowered counterpane up to Ellen's chin and plumped her pillows in a motherly fashion.

Turning on her side, Ellen tucked her hand beneath her cheek and yawned. "I don't know that I can explain how I feel, Becky. It is only that he seemed so distant in that moment, as though he weren't completely pleased."

Becky clicked her tongue. "Never you mind, miss. You've had a worrisome day, and no doubt you've fallen a bit into the sullens because you're so tired." And she began blowing out all the candles, the room slowly falling to darkness, except for a hazy pink glow emanating from a thick layer of coals piled up in the hearth.

Ellen closed her eyes, responding in a whisper, "I suppose I am very tired, but I feel so uneasy suddenly about Lord Bracknell."

In a low voice, Becky said, "I'm sure you'll feel quite differently after a good night's sleep."

And the door closed softly, the muffled sounds of her abigail's tread drifting into the night.

Chapter Seven

WHEN ELLEN AWOKE past noon, she found that Becky was right to a great degree after all. Her concerns, illumined by the clearer, steadier light of day, cast few shadows of significance, and she was able to dismiss them with scarcely a second thought. She saw nothing of the gentlemen that day or evening, for she had decided in accordance with Celeste's desires, to spend the remainder of the day in planning a shopping expedition for the following morning.

Both ladies bent their heads to the task with such energy, that before dinner had been served, the floors of both bedchambers resembled the aftermath of a strong wind on a forest of trees brimming with autumn leaves.

Nothing was to be left to chance, Ellen decided. And with Becky's strict approval, a new, more intriguing bevy of ball gowns, walking dresses, carriage dresses, pelisses, and bonnets was designed.

So it was with great excitement that the ladies faced the new day. Pulling on their gloves and tying the ribbons of their bonnets, they were about to depart from the town house when Jeremy and Laurence arrived.

"We could not stay away another minute," the gentlemen cried, laughing and exclaiming over the ladies' beauty. And upon discovering what Ellen and Celeste meant to do, they insisted upon attending them.

Ellen at first refused, but they teased and cajoled and

finally begged—in such a charming manner—to accompany the ladies on their adventure, that it was not long before Ellen acquiesced, especially when Celeste pressed her arm and cried, "Oh, but it would be such fun!"

As it turned out, the gentlemen were a delight, and as the town chariot bowled along New Bond Street, Ellen felt more content than she had in the past four days. She enjoyed the company of Bracknell's friends very much and thought they were a compliment to him. Even Laurie, for very soon they were on familiar terms, had set aside his scientific interests in order to entertain Celeste with several somewhat rakish anecdotes of events he had witnessed at the Five Courts and the Daffy Club.

They moved from shop to shop, ordering gowns here, gloves there and chatting with any number of their acquaintances along the way. Several times Ellen wondered if they would happen upon Lord Bracknell and whether or not she could be comfortable facing him after everything that had transpired at Vauxhall.

When they were nearly finished shopping and had but to order several bonnets, the small party found themselves inside a very cozy milliner's shop. There Ellen selected at least a dozen bonnets, much to her merriment, for the gentlemen approved and disapproved of every hat in turn and so noisily that they were all kept laughing. Jeremy was tying the ribbon of a bonnet beneath Ellen's chin, calling her a veritable wood nymph, and making her smile when Lord Bracknell's voice made them all stop in their movements. "What ho?" he called. "Playing the dandy, Mr. Andover, and judging the ladies' hats?"

Ellen turned and saw that Lord Bracknell had entered the shop with a tall, willowy female attached firmly to his arm. Ellen recognized the young lady as the viscount's cousin and felt an intense irritation spring to her breast at the mere sight of Mary Goodwin's noble features and proud bearing.

Having listened to Jeremy prattle on in the fine registers of his tenor voice and endured some of Laurie's flat monotones as he gauged the lengths of ribbons, the widths of brims, and the thickness of felt, Ellen realized how much even the timbre of Bracknell's voice seemed to have been designed to please her. He had a deep, rich voice, one that filled the milliner's shop and caused several females to turn interested heads his direction.

Mary, on the other hand, spoke in her habitually affected manner, which only increased Ellen's dislike of the simpering young lady. "But how charming, Miss Warfield," she said, "although the wide brim on that hat would certainly catch even the slightest breeze, and it would fly away from you!" Ellen watched as Miss Goodwin, her thin arm wrapped securely about Bracknell's own, turned to look up at her cousin and said, "Hugh, isn't Miss Warfield pretty? I have always thought the golden heiress casts the rest of us poor females quite in the shade."

Bracknell untwined his arm and said, "Indeed she does. I quite agree with you."

Laurence laughed outright, and Celeste moved to place an arm about her sister's waist in a protective manner that surprised Ellen. But she needn't have worried that Mary's attack would become overt. Mary was more concerned with keeping her cousin's attention fixed on herself. Her displeasure at Bracknell's defection was evident first in the scowl that passed across her features and then in the false smile she favored him with as she nipped his arm and said, "How cruel you are, when you know I was just begging for a compliment."

"At least you will admit it. I admire that, Mary. Now, do let us say good morning to our acquaintances."

"Oh, yes, let us."

Mary coquetted and smiled and kissed the air next to Ellen's cheek, nodded to Celeste, shook hands with Jeremy and Laurence, proclaimed her raptures over the bonnets they had declined to purchase, and pursed her lips over the hats they meant to take home with them, pinched at Bracknell about a trifling headache that had begun to overtake her, and finally sat sullenly in a rosewood chair of lavender needlepoint, holding her vinaigrette to her nose.

Ellen ignored her and thought the better of Lord Bracknell for also ignoring his cousin. She was particularly pleased with the very obvious effort he made to engage her in conversation, commenting upon her excellent choice of bonnets. Had she imagined it or had Bracknell seemed the least bit irritable when he entered the shop and took in the very cozy picture of Jeremy tying her bonnet on? And had the barest hint of jealousy crossed his features?

When Mary could no longer tolerate being ignored, she snapped her gold vinaigrette shut and stuffed it back in her reticule. Rising to her feet, she said, "Cousin, dearest, I know it is dreadfully inconvenient, but I have a fierce headache and must return home at once. Although, even the fresh air achieved by riding in your curricle might revive me sufficiently."

Bracknell turned to regard her and said, "I have little doubt the fresh air will restore your health entirely."

Mary bit her lip and refused to be baited into saying more but waited for him to begin his adieus.

Ellen wanted to laugh, but at that moment, Bracknell lifted her gloved hand to his lips and kissed her fingers. What was it about the man that kept her emotions so near the surface, for he had but to salute her fingers and her surroundings faded from view. She saw only him, Jeremy's laughter and Celeste's polite good-byes to Mary becoming a mere drone as Bracknell met her gaze. His hazel eyes sparkled with their habitual mischief. Merciful heavens, he was so very handsome, Ellen thought. She felt her heart strain toward him, toward some part of him that seemed to be like her. And much to her horror, she felt the strongest compulsion to hold onto him, to keep him near her. She looked away from him at that moment. Never, she decided, would she let a man possess her heart in such a fashion. Why, Mary obviously felt that way, nearly strangling him with her presence—as though he could ever love a woman like that! Oh, why was this all so complicated?

The moment passed, and before Ellen knew what had happened, the little silver bell dangling on a cord attached to the back of the door announced the cousins had departed.

Laurie held his quizzing glass up to his eye, picked up a long ostrich feather, and pointing it swordlike toward the door, danced forward several times as though he were fencing. "Seemed rather miffed, did he not? Jeremy, I don't think he liked Miss Warfield's bonnet. To be precise, I don't think he cared for your hands being on Miss Warfield's bonnet."

Both men laughed gaily, and Celeste turned to nod in an encouraging, I-told-you-so fashion toward Ellen. However, Ellen was not certain what to think, for she had a gnawing sensation that if she did not take great care, she would lose both her heart and her pride to Lord Bracknell. And not for the world did she wish to become a vinelike, clinging creature such as Mary Goodwin was, keeping her arms laced about a man's coat sleeves as though her entire existence depended upon his smiles of approval.

The next few days—it was actually a week, Ellen realized with an increasing sense of alarm—blended together in a haze of soirees and grand balls, excursions to Hyde Park, and even a visit to the Tower to see the lions exhibited there. And though Lord Bracknell and his companions in arms had escorted them on at least a dozen different occasions, besides calling upon them nearly every afternoon, Ellen could not be content. Especially when she realized a mere eighteen days remained in which to bring Bracknell up to scratch. The task before her again seemed impossible.

Lord Bracknell was certainly attentive, and to a large degree she thought he enjoyed her company, but there was a reserve about him she found nearly impossible to penetrate. As she dressed for the opera, where she and Celeste were to join the gentlemen in Lord Bracknell's box, a strong sense of panic assailed her, and she shook her head feeling even Venus herself would be unable to extract a proposal of marriage from the viscount. How was it her papa had thought she could do it? Surely he had gone mad just before he had set down such conditions to his will. Surely!

As she pulled on her white gloves, Ellen regarded the

telegraph fan resting upon her dressing table. Her father had given it to her more than a month before he died, and of the moment, she could not quite remember how the fan had come up in conversation with the gentlemen. But the result was that Laurence had requested to see the unusual fan, which supposedly had been used during the revolt in France to convey secret messages through the manipulation of the spokes—each of which represented a letter of the alphabet.

Ellen sighed, picking up the fan and securing it in her reticule, and wondered just how she was to make the viscount fall in love with her.

From the moment they entered Lord Bracknell's box at the Royal Italian Opera House in the Haymarket, a madcap progression of friends, acquaintances, and even a few enemies streamed in and out—from every manner of puppy bowing low over Ellen's hand and causing Bracknell to laugh at her, to several half-foxed Corinthians asking whether or not the viscount had been to Jackson's Boxing Saloon lately.

In between visitors, Laurie examined Ellen's fan, trying to determine precisely how the spokes were manipulated and whether or not Ellen had gained competence in spelling out words with it.

Ellen was just then shaking her head in the negative, when Lady Jersey, one of the haut ton's more formidable hostesses, entered the box. "There you are, my dear Bracknell. So you are finally gracing our society again—and that with someone we might acknowledge." She inclined her head to Ellen. "And how do you do, Miss Warfield?"

"Very well, thank you, ma'am."

Lady Jersey raised a brow as she scanned Ellen's gown and pronounced, "That particular shade of blue is unbecoming someone of your tender years. I recommend white or a pale pink for ladies just out."

Ellen smiled politely, refusing to argue with a woman who was ironically known as "Silence" among the beau monde, and Lady Jersey turned her attention back to the viscount.

Lord Bracknell rose and begged her ladyship to be seated, but she waved her fan of mother-of-pearl about her in an imperious fashion, saying she rather preferred to stand and demanding to know when he would be attending the assemblies at Almack's. "For you are by far too marriageable a creature to be left to your own devices, and what, pray tell, is all this nonsense I have had heard about your actually having mortgaged Three Elms?"

Ellen's attention became fixed intently upon Bracknell's face, for Lady Jersey's questions had struck so nearly to the heart of her own concerns that she held her breath as she waited for the viscount to respond.

Lord Bracknell removed his snuffbox from his coat pocket and took a pinch. "As to the first, I fear were I to give you my opinions of Almack's, you would shun me forever, and that I could not bear—"

"The little cakes are always stale, but that is Countess Lieven's fault—it certainly isn't mine!"

"—and as to your second question, why, you've always known I am fond of gaming." And he regarded her with a mischievous smile playing about his lips.

Lady Jersey narrowed her eyes at him. "Yes, but what game are you playing now, for never will I believe for one moment you would risk losing your ancestral properties to a game of dice or cards. But I must return to my box, for the orchestra has set up that familiar screeching sound—why could they not tune their instruments beforehand!"

"Ah, if you could but manage the entire country, my dear Sally—"

Lady Jersey rapped his arm soundly with her fan and turned her attention to Ellen. In a voice full of disapproval, she said, "And I do not think, Miss Warfield, even though your sister is a matron, she is quite suitable to be chaperoning you anywhere, and especially not with Lord Bracknell. Why, you and Mrs. Hazeley are both scarcely out of the schoolroom! And I am certain Vincent would never have approved. Your sister is by far too young to be deemed an appropriate chaperon, and I do not hesitate to say you run the very great risk of offending some of our high sticklers. As it happens, I have a cousin, a woman of unexceptionable breeding, accepted in our highest circles, who can lend you the proper countenance while you are here in London. I shall send her to you in the morning." And she nodded as if the subject were closed.

Ellen smiled sweetly and replied, "Pray do not, for I, too, have several aging cousins who I fear would disown me forever were I to offer so consequential a position to a complete stranger."

Lady Jersey gasped. "How very impertinent you are become! If it weren't for Vincent, I should rescind your vouchers to Almack's."

Lord Bracknell laughed aloud at this exchange, much to Lady Jersey's disapproval. And when she had left, he whispered to Ellen, "I admire your courage! Such a dragon!"

"She is harmless; just . . . just a trifle managing."

Bracknell regarded her steadily. "Like you. Very managing. But how were you able to speak like that, in so forthright a manner, to a female who causes even Mary to turn white and stammer as though she were a schoolgirl. Are you not afraid of anything, Miss Warfield?"

There it was again, that very curious spark in his eye, as though he knew a joke so amusing, no matter how terrible the circumstances, he would always be able to smile. She liked him. Heaven help her, she liked him very much. And suddenly she knew a way to his heart, a path full of irony, for it involved not simperings and cajolings, but something far more difficult—revealing her own heart to him.

She trembled at the thought. What if he laughed at her, or worse, merely shrugged his shoulders in a care-for-nobody manner? The overture to *Don Giovanni* began, and Ellen steeled herself, remembering yet again her Papa's will and Warfield Hall. Her heart hammering in her ears, Ellen leaned quite close to him and met his slightly amused gaze. In a whisper, she said, "I am afraid of many things,

Lord Bracknell. And in particular, I am afraid of you, of losing my heart to you."

And as quickly as the words were spoken Ellen averted her gaze. Her hands felt very cold, and her heart still pounded desperately in her ears as she turned her attention to the opera commencing on the stage below. Why had she spoken so brazenly? Why had she exposed herself to him?

Bracknell stole a glance at Ellen's profile and thought with every day that advanced he was becoming more and more tangled in a dreadful coil. Faith, but he found himself drawn to her and now this. She had spoken sincerely, her green eyes indeed appearing stricken, as though she were afraid he would hurt her, and by God, he could. How very much these words had cost her, he realized, for they were both alike in one thing—neither of them lifted the veil to his thoughts or emotions without great effort.

The odd thing was this opinion of hers, in essence that she did not trust him, troubled him deeply. In a dozen small things she had said over the past several days, she had made her low opinion of gamesters in general, and himself in particular, quite obvious. But he wasn't a gamester—gad, what a coil! For the life of him, he could not quite comprehend why, Ellen's trust was fast becoming his goal.

Laurence, who was seated behind Ellen, leaned forward and slipped the telegraph fan to her, whispering that he found it quite fascinating and were it his own, he would take it apart in order to examine it in detail. Lord Bracknell regarded the fan as Ellen held it clasped in her hands, and again felt slightly overwhelmed at the web of deceit he was weaving. For even the fact that she had brought her telegraph fan to the opera had been a direct manipulation of his—he had purposely brought the subject forward not two days ago at Hyde Park in front of Laurence, who he knew would be instantly intrigued by the idea that such an article had ever existed. The budding scientist did not disappoint him, and Laurie's enthusiasm had quickly stolen the day as he begged Ellen to bring it to the opera on Friday so he might have a look at it. Bracknell sincerely doubted Ellen would even remember he was the one who had originated the conversation. But just how much confidence would she have in him then once she learned he had tricked her out of three very personal possessions? And he sighed heavily, wishing he had never met Vincent Warfield.

During the intermission the entire opera house resounded with a thousand conversations being conducted simultaneously. Ellen handed her fan to the viscount upon his request, her heart beating in odd jumps and starts. She wondered what he would next say to her and if he would ask her what she had meant by telling him she was afraid of him.

"Ingenious!" Bracknell pronounced, turning the fan over in his hands several times. "And are you able to operate it? Do you have conspirators with whom you exchange secrets?"

"Oh, no. I haven't mastered it at all, and I know of no one else who possesses one," Ellen replied, grateful they were conversing about something as harmless as her fan. But what was he thinking? Had her own admission of the power he held over her affected him in the least? As she studied his face, his gaze cast downward upon the fan, she experienced a sudden longing that surprised her, and she looked away from him quickly. Watching him spreading open the fan and trying to move each spoke, Ellen wondered what she ought to do next, when a familiar voice caused her to wince.

Ambrose stood at the doorway of the box. "I did not credit my eyes, but here you are before me, my dear wife!" And he moved forward, placing his hands upon Celeste's shoulders, and squeezing them hard. "Why did you not tell me you had come to London? You are being very sly."

Ellen turned around and saw Celeste's face twist in pain as she gave a sudden cry. "Ambrose, pray do not be angry!" Celeste begged. Ellen was furious her cousin would dare to cause such a scene and prepared to do battle herself at the sight of his cruelty. But before she could take action, Jeremy leapt from his seat, his face flushed, his brown eyes sporting a fiery expression as he cried, "Remove your hands at once, or you shall answer to me for it!" And he stepped toward Ambrose, his fists clenched.

Ambrose released his wife, and Celeste rose immediately from her seat, placing her hands protectively against Jeremy's chest. "No!" she cried. "Pray do not provoke him, Jeremy! He will kill you!"

Both men had put their hands quite symbolically upon invisible sword hilts, and the surrounding boxes erupted with gasps and exclamations. Ellen's imagination traveled quickly from the opera house to secretive discussions among chosen seconds to a misty morning upon some forbidden heath to Jeremy lying prone and bleeding from a wound to the head.

Ellen shook her head, and the horrifying images disappeared. No one moved. She could see Jeremy would follow the business through to the end to defend Celeste, and Ellen had an uneasy feeling his reactions were overly strong for only having known her sister for a mere fortnight or more.

Ambrose's eyes shifted suddenly as he glanced quickly about until he caught sight of the fan Lord Bracknell still held in his hands. A funny light darted through his eyes, and his gaze returned to Jeremy. He laughed lightly, taking a step backward and lifting his quizzing glass to view his wife. Celeste still had her hands on Jeremy's coat, keeping him away from her husband.

Ambrose said, "I apologize, my dear, if I hurt you. I wouldn't for the world cause you pain. But then, you were always so very fragile, were you not?" He surveyed his wife's gloved hands touching the handsome poet in an appearance of intimacy. Lifting an ironic brow, he remarked, "I daresay you are crushing the lapel of Mr. Andover's coat. I shouldn't do that if I were you. You will set a crease, and no doubt his valet will be in tears for a week." He seemed to ignore the disgusted grunt erupting from Jeremy's lips and the blush diffusing over Celeste's cheeks as she removed her hands and lowered them in something of a maidenly confusion to her sides.

Ambrose then progressed further into the box, ignoring his wife, the pink bows and dangling ribbons adorning his white-satin knee breeches dancing as he minced forward. "Ah, Ellen," he cried, "It is you I came to see most particularly." And he moved past the back row toward her.

Ellen heard Celeste arguing with Jeremy, begging him to sit down and not to provoke her husband, who was a known duelist of great skill. From the corner of her eye she watched the poet slump in his chair, his arms folded over his chest, a scowl on his face. Celeste sat down as well, her face hidden behind her fan.

Ellen scanned her cousin's pomaded locks and the enormous quizzing glass that hung from a long silk riband and now dangled to his waist, and revulsion twisted her stomach. How could Celeste ever have loved such a creature? As the various personages in the boxes next to them resumed their own activities, Ellen spoke in a low angry voice, "What do you want, you faithless blackguard!"

"Why, nothing of import, m'dear. Merely to assure myself you are well." He glanced in a meaningful fashion at Lord Bracknell and again stole a glimpse of the fan. Feigning surprise, he cried, "Good heavens, could that possibly be a telegraph fan? Why, I have wished to see one for ages! May I look at it?"

Ellen was furious her cousin had treated his wife with such great disrespect and afterward appeared as though nothing out of the ordinary had occurred. Still keeping her voice low, she cried, "No! You may not so much as touch it, and I do not hesitate to inform you are not welcome here."

He laughed again, as though Ellen were being quite silly, and started to sit down when Bracknell said, "I wouldn't if I were you, Mr. Hazeley." His voice was hard and commanding and, unlike Ellen, he did not speak in a guarded tone. "The ladies have taken offense to your presence, and I won't have it. You may bow politely and leave. Anything more, the merest lift of a brow, and I shall be most happy to throw you from the balcony." He finished with a smile.

Ellen sat straighter in her chair, eyeing the viscount with what she was certain was a rather gaping expression. Here was a man who did not mince words. She liked this about him almost as much as she liked the suddenly hard cast to his hazel eyes. In this case, all the laughter was gone, and in its stead was firmness and resolve, an expression she had often seen holding court in her father's eyes.

She turned to scrutinize Ambrose, wondering what he thought of this direct attack and noticed her cousin's gaze had again shifted to the fan Bracknell still held clasped lightly in his hands. He seemed rather torn in that moment, his eyes flickering back to Ellen's face, and appeared uncertain if he should take Bracknell at his word.

Ellen could not resist adding, "Yes, do go away, Ambrose. Your pink ribbons offend me!" And she tugged at one of the bows that adorned the knees of his satin breeches, and released the feminine ribbons so they streamed next to the large clocks embroidered on his stockings. What a tulip her cousin had become.

Ambrose glanced down at the loose ribbons and then glowered at Ellen, his green-gold eyes dark with anger. "Ever the child!" he snapped. And in a sweeping motion, he bowed, mocking them all, and finally quit the viscount's box.

Ellen felt her hands begin to tremble. How stupid! She should not let her cousin upset her so, but he represented so many despicable things to her that even when he was charming and polite, his mere presence was an irritation. But this—treating his wife with such cruelty—was unbearable. She clasped her hands together tightly, hoping Bracknell would not notice how greatly she was affected, and said, "Oh, dear. He is something of a cretin, is he not?" She smiled slightly at the viscount, who very gently placed his hand over hers. He held her gaze and said, "The merest puppy. Pray don't let him spoil your evening."

There it was again, his sweetness and consideration, always so at odds with his careful reserve. She felt an inexplicable weakness wash over her. How well he seemed to understand her. In a quiet voice, she responded, "I hope

I am never so foolish as to allow my cousin to affect my enjoyment of anything." She looked back at her sister, who was now deep in conversation with Jeremy.

Ellen felt Bracknell draw back his hand, and she again studied him, thoughtfully. In a low voice, she said, "You must permit me to thank you for giving my cousin so little ground. How might I repay you?" Even as she spoke these words she felt Becky would certainly have approved. Her maid had spoken strongly about binding the gentleman to her by being constantly in his debt. "Never stop thanking him for even the smallest kindness."

Bracknell was still holding the telegraph fan, and just as he was about to open his mouth and play the gentlemen and refute the need for repayment, he remembered his duty. Somewhere among Ellen's acquaintance was a traitor to England. As he leaned close to Ellen he tapped her hands lightly with the telegraph fan, and asked, "Would you entrust your fan to me, Miss Warfield?"

Ellen viewed him with surprise. "You want my fan?" And she glanced down at her hands, where the collapsed spokes were making little circles upon her white gloves. She could almost laugh as she remembered another bit of Becky's advice. "Saddle a gentleman with your trifles, that he might be forced to remember you every time he casts his eyes upon them."

Bracknell nodded, his hazel eyes again glinting with mischief, as he replied, "Yes, as a reward for my valor in fending off your cousin. Faith, what a fire-eater. You indeed ought to extol my bravery, for I vow I was shaking in my boots."

Ellen leaned back in her chair, knowing full well he was teasing her, and cried, "What a whisker!" As she peered at his face, she suddenly realized his eyes were again very bright, just as they had been at Vauxhall when he had first seen the gold-embroidered kerchief. A funny dart of suspicion crossed Ellen's mind, and she again experienced that same quirky, uneasy feeling that had assailed her the moment she had given her kerchief into Bracknell's safekeeping.

Regarding the viscount askance, she frowned at him, and continued, "I suppose I have no choice in the matter, since I offered to repay you, but I think I shall pose to you the same question Lady Jersey asked earlier: What game are you playing, my lord?"

Chapter Eight

LORD BRACKNELL DID not see Ellen on Saturday. On Sunday morning he awoke with a mouth that felt stuffed full of cotton. His head ached, and he swore when this particular service to his country was over, he would retire, permanently. He rolled out of bed, planted his feet on the floor, and tried to stand, but a shot of pain nearly took the top of his head off, and he sat down on the bed again. He had been to five gaming establishments on the night before, flaunting his possession of both Ellen's fan and her kerchief.

Cradling his head in his hands, he squeezed his eyes shut, not wanting to think about the truth he had uncovered. He was nearly certain now who Vincent had planned to expose, and he still couldn't believe it was true. No wonder Warfield had insisted upon so much secrecy, for the suspect was none other than Ambrose Hazeley. Good God! Celeste's husband, Ellen's cousin, Vincent's nephew and son-in-law. What a terrible scandal there would be—if indeed it was true.

At Mrs. Stratfield's gaming establishment, the last place where Bracknell had posed as a hardened gamester, Ambrose had approached him, apologizing for his conduct at the opera. They'd been playing at hazard, a rather raucous crowd of ladies and gentlemen lining the table, and Bracknell had displayed the fan and the kerchief quite prominently, telling anyone who would listen that he had conquered the golden heiress and that her trifles would bring him a great deal of luck. And so it proved, for after he flung the dice across the green baize, the crowd groaning and cheering in accordance with their bets, the viscount saw what he had been waiting to see. Only why did it have to be Hazeley staring intently at both objects, his green-gold eyes sharp and rather dilated, his lips parted slightly.

Of course it made sense, Bracknell thought. A gamester, deeply in debt, someone known to Ellen—too well known. Gad, what a coil. He now had only to acquire the snuffbox and to prove to himself that Ambrose was indeed the man he was after and he could bring this dastardly business to a rapid conclusion. He thought he might try to involve Ambrose in the acquisition of the snuffbox—perhaps he would invite Ellen to Mrs. Stratfield's gaming establishment, somehow making certain Ambrose would know of it.

How simple it was to scheme and plan, how easy it was to manipulate events and people, but what of Ellen and her sensibilities, for she was being treated as a mere pawn in this desperate game. Damme, he cared for her. And if she ever discovered just how he had bandied her name about, he would have the devil of a time trying to regain her confidence.

Bracknell's valet, Huntspill appeared with shaving gear in hand to scrape a layer of debauched stubble from his chin. Bracknell took comfort in the knowledge that in but a few hours he was to escort Ellen to Hyde Park, and no one could possibly have informed against him in so short a period of time.

That afternoon, however, he realized his error. As he seated himself beside Ellen in his black curricle and dispatched his horses she immediately asked him, her green eyes sparkling with anger, just precisely what he hoped to gain by boasting to the entire beau monde that he was now in possession of her kerchief and fan.

Ellen twisted her parasol in a hand that seemed to have a life of its own as she listened to Bracknell's soft explanation. "I daresay you have no reason to forgive me," he said "but I hope you will. and I did not precisely boast of possessing your fan—"

"You didn't? But Lady Jersey heard you." Scarcely an hour earlier, Sally Jersey had called upon Ellen and most kindly regaled her with the viscount's perfidy. Her words still stung as Ellen recalled them. "So, Lord Bracknell has quite taken a fancy to you, has he? Tell me, is it true he captured your fan from you? He was telling everyone at Mrs. Stratfield's charming little gaming establishment that he won your heart and fan in a single stroke, at the opera, if I remember the story correctly, and that he was certain the golden heiress would be the answer to all his current strivings with the local cent-percenters. It is all so very intriguing, Miss Warfield. What can it mean? I hope you have not fallen victim to Bracknell's charms!"

Ellen shuddered as she remembered the superior expression on Lady Jersey's face, and now Bracknell insisted upon treating the matter lightly.

Bracknell frowned slightly as he said, "So my Lady Jersey has become a tattle-monger. But I hope you will pay no heed to what she says to you. As it happens, I was not boasting at all; rather, I was flaunting possession of your fan—quite a different matter entirely."

Ellen played with the fringe of her pink parasol. "I cannot imagine what you mean. What precisely is the difference between boasting and flaunting?"

He softly called his horses to a halt, sitting very straight in his seat, the reigns held lightly in his gloved hands. "If I had been boasting, it would have meant a sort of pride in conquering your heart. But since I was *flaunting* the fan, I meant only to express an immense pleasure that you had entrusted it to me."

Ellen looked up to scrutinize his profile, a rueful smile on her lips. "What humbug!" she cried. "And don't think you can turn me up sweet, for I am very much aggrieved by you. Had I known you would have displayed my kerchief or my fan before the world, I would never have given them to you!"

The bays were snorting loudly and stamping their feet,

impatient to be moving again, but Lord Bracknell held them in check as he regarded Ellen with a smile. "If I promise never to do so again, would you forgive me this one lapse in gentlemanly conduct?"

Ellen's gaze was fixed quite firmly upon her parasol. She tried not to smile, but she couldn't help it. He had bewitched her; she was certain of that now. She had indeed fallen victim to Lord Bracknell's charms for quite against either her will or her common sense, she would forgive him—drat the man. And he deserved no such consideration from her!

A strong gust of wind nearly lifted Ellen's new bonnet from her head—the very one Mary Goodwin had prophesied over—and she laughed aloud. Pressing her hat firmly against the crown of her head, she cried, "Oh, pray set your horses in motion. The wind sweeps across the square at this time of day and will certainly put your horses on the fret." Glancing up at him, she added in a quieter voice, "And . . . and I wish to hear nothing more of my fan or my kerchief."

He nodded to her with an approving expression that added a burst of hope to Ellen's heart. Searching his face a moment, she noted his strong chin and the amusement that was never far from his soft hazel eyes. Faith, but she liked him.

They spoke of everything and of nothing. Of Turner's exhibit at the Royal Academy and the ridiculous height at which many of the paintings were hung. Of Wellington's exploits in Portugal and of the latest fashion of putting large, fringed epaulets on the shoulders of ladies' pelisses. Of Laurie's propensity toward gaming and Jeremy's hopes of one day attaining the fame Lord Byron had so recently achieved. Of everything, of nothing, a delightful ease between them, like friends chatting before a warm, crackling fire at a friendly inn, where the apples are golden and the brandy very old.

Sunday merged into Monday, then Tuesday, and the week passed as every day brought the viscount round to Berkeley Square, with Jeremy and Laurence often in tow.

The entire party moved happily from fete to soiree.

Finally, Bracknell managed to maneuver the group to Mrs. Stratfield's gaming establishment. Laurie tutored Ellen in all the mysteries of hazard—she found herself charmed by the dice—and Jeremy took Celeste to play at roulette. Lord Bracknell remained by the hazard table watching Ellen and delighting in her enjoyment of the game. But as he regarded Ellen he couldn't help thinking of her father's gold snuffbox secreted within the reticule dangling upon her wrist. A sadness crept up on him as he remembered that very soon the tenor of the evening would shift when Ambrose arrived.

His schemes nearly always worked to perfection, for he left nothing to chance. He had purposely sought out Ambrose at Boodle's during the past week and dropped a hint that he meant to introduce Ellen to the Stratfield rooms. And in that moment the shaft of greed that darted through the gamester's eyes, laid all Bracknell's doubts to rest. Ambrose was his man.

The worst part of the business was manipulating Ellen. Feigning a profound interest in snuffboxes in general, and gold ones specifically, had taken every ounce of his energy, particularly in the face of Ellen's enthusiasm for her papa's box. How would all his schemes, however noble in terms of his country's future, affect Ellen? When she learned he had been using her, would she ever forgive him? But more to the point, he thought suddenly, why had it become of supreme importance to him that Ellen hold him in high esteem? He shook his head, unable to comprehend the sense of urgency he felt on this score.

Turning his attention back to Ellen, he saw she was feverishly caught in a thrilling game of hazard. She had nicked it ten times in a row and had the entire crowd cheering for her, her brow flushed prettily with beads of perspiration. Here was a side to her he had not seen before. With each throw she would set aside a quarter of her winnings—much to the annoyance of every truly hardened gamester in the place, but much to his own delight—so that before her rested two piles of pound notes. Nearly two thousand pounds.

Laurence stood beside her quoting odds and telling her how to hedge her bets so she almost couldn't lose. Ellen slipped her arm through Laurie's and begged him to tell her precisely what she should do. Lord Bracknell watched this friendly motion and felt a very odd tightening sensation in his chest. He knew it was foolish, for indeed all five of them had become fast friends, but he still felt an impulse to speak with Mr. Chawton about taking such grievous advantage of Vincent Warfield's daughter. Immediately, he laughed at himself. For who among the three gentlemen had kissed her half a dozen times, not to mention made every effort to undo her heart? An odd realization, this, and for a moment he thought he was actually developing a rather silly tendre for the chit.

Impossible! He was far beyond the age or predilection for falling in love. And certainly not with Ellen Warfield, a mere chit of a girl!

But she was hardly a chit, he thought as he scanned the emeralds glistening about her neck and on her hand. And the décolleté gown scarcely bespoke a schoolgirl. He would admit he was particularly enamored of her gold curls, now wound throughout with a ribbon the precise shade of pink bramble flowers.

He was reminded suddenly of seeing her on the back terrace of Warfield Hall several years ago, a woven basket over her arm, long, fingerless gloves keeping the sun from marring her bare skin. Later she brought several dozen roses into the hall, a smile full of summer on her face. She had been very young at the time, still in the schoolroom. He had only recently begun his work with Vincent and had stopped at Warfield Hall for a short time in order to review his latest assignment involving brandy smugglers near Bristol who were thought to have been transporting French spies. Vincent had caught his daughter, pulling two long gold curls hanging down to the middle of her back. Ellen for her part had teased her papa mercilessly, and Warfield had loved every minute of it. Bracknell remembered the charm of the moment, the feisty, amusing relationship father and daughter had enjoyed and how beautiful Ellen was, much like the roses she carried.

He became aware suddenly, as the crowd gave a cheer, that he was staring at her. And just in that moment, she lifted her sparkling gaze, eyes as green as the emeralds about her white throat, and smiled at him. She kissed the dice as she held his gaze—faith, but had she kissed his own lips, he could not have felt the pressure of her lips more strongly. She was brimming with excitement and life and everything he had ever wanted in a female. The dice danced out of Ellen's hand, and she nicked it again, the crowd cheering her on.

As the spectators roared in response and the pound notes flew across the table, Ellen impulsively kissed Laurie's cheek, who in turn blushed darkly, his freckles merging together, and then looked sheepishly, but with great affection, upon his protégé.

This time the hard sensation that had just a moment earlier strangled Bracknell's chest now moved upward to his throat. Draining his glass of Madeira he gave it to a passing servant and left the side of the table to join Laurie and Ellen at the end.

"Bracknell!" Ellen cried. "How grateful I am you brought me here!" She then whispered to him that with such earnings she might not have to marry after all and smiled brightly upon him.

Ellen again separated a quarter of her winnings from the rest, kissed the dice, and rolled them gaily across the green baize. Crabs—a two and a three. The crowd groaned, and Ellen frowned at the ivory traitors staring back at her.

Laurie rubbed the side of his nose and said, "Jinxed her, Hugh. Not very sporting, what?"

Ellen laughed as she picked up the remaining pound notes and after organizing her newly acquired largess into a neat pile, she rolled up the pound notes carefully and placed them in a small knit purse, which in turn she tucked into her reticule. Bracknell was amused at such a sense of order.

"Oh, stuff and nonsense, Laurie!" Ellen cried. "It was never my money anyway. And I am still taking away more than I should, more than anyone should. And whose money have I won is what I should like to know. Who has lost it? Why, I feel as though I am stealing!"

Laurie appeared shocked. "Never say it! A gentleman's game, gambling."

Bracknell smiled at Ellen's quaint philosophy, but said nothing about it. He was afraid to, for he was certain if he opened his mouth he would call her a darling and perhaps a dozen other things he wasn't at all certain he wished to say. Instead, he asked if she would like to play the foreign game of roulette, also called *rouge et noir*. The idea enchanted Ellen, and within minutes they were fully involved in all the intricacies of reds and blacks.

After some thirty minutes had passed and Ellen's previous winnings had dwindled rapidly, Bracknell lifted his gaze to glance about the table, wondering when Hazeley would arrive. A little to his surprise he discovered Ambrose standing but a few feet away from Ellen and watching her intently. The moment had come, he realized with a sudden depression of his spirits, to put the last sequence of Vincent's plan into effect. He was struck with the thought that his time so closely linked with Ellen was drawing to an end, and that he did not want it to, but he set these thoughts firmly aside and took a quick measure of the situation.

Ellen was in the midst of laying a pound note on the table, when he stopped her hand, and said, "Would you care to place a wager with me, Miss Warfield? You have something I long to possess—a gold snuffbox."

Her startled expression was not lost to him, and he could see from the corner of his eye how Hazeley started at his words. Had exposing himself so completely to the enemy been wise? He wondered.

Ellen clutched her reticule tightly, feeling the small rectangular box through the pearl-embroidered silk, her heart quickening suddenly. Bracknell had shown a great deal of interest in her father's snuffbox over the last few days, even mentioning once that he had always admired Vincent, but she was still surprised that he wished to possess it. She blinked several times, her thoughts moving rapidly through her mind, and a familiar uneasiness again resting on her heart.

"What an interesting wager," Ambrose remarked.

Ellen heard her cousin's voice, and nearly jumped as she turned to find him standing next to her. "What are you doing here, Ambrose?"

He merely lifted his brow.

Ellen said, "Does Mrs. Stratfield actually permit you to punt upon tick?"

His brows shot up at this. "Vulgarisms, Ellen? But then, they do roll prettily from your lips. Pray, don't let me interrupt so fascinating a game."

The few people about the roulette table, several in their cups, began laying bets before Ellen ever agreed to the wager. She searched her cousin's visage for a moment. She was trying to remember something he had said about a snuffbox just a fortnight ago—something about her papa's gold snuffbox.

She turned to peer at Bracknell to try to determine what she ought to do, but his gaze was fixed on Ambrose, his expression somewhat malevolent. No doubt, he was wondering if she wished her cousin thrown bodily from the town house.

Realizing the viscount's hand was still pressed over hers, she knew she had to come to a decision quickly. But how was she to decide precisely what to do? Bracknell already possessed both her fan and her kerchief. How could she give the snuffbox up? As the question formed itself in her mind, the answer was almost as speedily present—if she didn't win Bracknell's hand in marriage over the next week, she would be losing a great deal more than one rather battered snuffbox.

She straightened slightly, and with her heart beating loudly in her breast, asked, "And what, my lord, will you stake in return? I should inform you that being extremely wealthy, I have everything I could possibly want."

Much to the great interest of those players who enjoyed following the golden heiress about and betting at her games, Lord Bracknell answered, "Anything you desire of me."

Ellen's heart raced suddenly at the possibilities of such a wager. She could ask for his hand in marriage, and as a gentleman, he would have to give it to her. "Done!" she cried.

Ellen watched an expression of amusement cross his features, and he released her hand, whispering, "You intrigue me. And what, I wonder, could I possibly give you that has caused your eyes to positively glow."

Averting her gaze as bets were laid and the wheel began to spin, Ellen responded, "I shan't tell you." She then prayed the little ball would find the proper home. How long it took for the wheel to slow, the ball clattering, and finally falling into a space. Her space. Ellen could have shouted with sheer joy. It was over. She would demand his hand in marriage, and Lord Bracknell, as a gentleman of honor, and before these many witnesses, would be forced to agree to her demands!

Forced to agree to her demands. How deeply the thought struck her, hammering her sudden joy to a flat little nothing. She did not wish to force him to do anything. She wanted him to love her, to want her more than he had ever wanted any female. Because . . . because she loved him!

She felt his hand on her arm and knew he had started to speak in his habitually light tone, amusement in his voice: *what did she wish, he was hers to command*. But Ellen was so consumed with her own thoughts of how impossible her situation was that she wheeled away from him, bumping into Ambrose and then pushing past him. The crowd whispered behind her, but she didn't care. She knew the despicable truth—she was hopelessly in love with a man who could not return her love—and all she wanted at the moment was to be alone.

She heard him calling to her, following her through the maze of anterooms, each with its own card party in progress. She wished she did not have to face him. She dreaded seeing the amusement in his eyes. He was always amused with her, and he even seemed as though he enjoyed being with her—for the moment. But in time, he would grow bored, and would disappear, returning to haunt the theaters again, where he would dazzle the cyprians with his smiles. Oh, she hated him, hated this business. Her pride was dashed against the rocks of his practiced flirtations. He had conquered her so thoroughly.

"Ellen." His voice sounded bemused. He caught up with her as she stopped in her tracks, pretending to decide whether she should join a table of whist players or return to the hazard table. "What is it?" he asked. "What is the matter?" He caught her elbow and turned her gently about, forcing her to face him.

Ellen did not wish to look at him, at the concern creasing his brow, at the dreaded warmth of his hazel eyes.

"I didn't mean to upset you. It was a mistake. I should never have suggested such a wager," he said as he pulled her away from the constant flow of people about the rooms into the recesses of an ill-lit corner. He took her chin gently in hand and said, "I have hurt you. What is wrong?"

Ellen stared into his eyes, the shadows softening his penetrating gaze. She shook her head. "I've been very foolish. What I want from you, you are unable to give."

He gazed deeply into her eyes, his expression suddenly intense. "You need a husband."

"Yes," she said. "I need a husband. But if I marry, would I gain love? I think not."

He released her chin, but he still held her arm as though afraid she would bolt. Ellen felt her heart race as a very strange expression passed over his features. He seemed struck by an idea completely novel in form, and a dart of hope threatened to undo her.

"Ellen," he said in a whisper, as he leaned closer to her. She could almost feel his breath on her cheek.

She waited, and her heart told her he was about to speak the words she wanted so desperately to hear.

But Celeste's voice, trembling with fear, intruded. "Ellen! Ambrose is here. Pray, let us go at once. I fear for

Jeremy! And . . . and he wishes to speak with me in private!"

Turning away from Bracknell, Ellen saw the look of hurt and confusion on her sister's face and immediately slipped an arm about her waist. "What for? What can he possibly want?"

"I don't know; it is just that I am afraid. Oh, please, let us go!" She pulled on Ellen's arm, but Jeremy was upon them suddenly, with Ambrose closely on his heels.

Drawing very close to Celeste, the fire-eating poet glared at Ambrose and started to speak, but Ambrose cut him off. "I mean no harm, I assure you. I merely wish to speak with Celeste. Is that so very much to ask? She is, after all, my wife!"

Ellen saw that the situation could explode, and she spoke quickly, before the poet could give vent to his animosity toward Ambrose. "Call upon us tomorrow at eleven, Cousin. But, pray, leave us now!"

He looked as though he wished to speak, but after seeing how Jeremy's brown eyes darkened even as he looked at him, he merely bowed and walked slowly away.

Celeste leaned heavily against Jeremy, who slipped an arm about her shoulder and began consoling her while she wept into a kerchief drawn hastily from her reticule.

Ellen watched them for a moment, listening to the tender words flowing from Jeremy's lips, and her heart nearly stopped beating. Jeremy loved Celeste, and obviously the sentiment was reciprocated by her sister. She had suspected as much, but she had been so caught up in her own concerns that she had not paid very much attention to just how far matters had progressed between them.

And what of Bracknell's, she wondered suddenly as she glanced up at the viscount. What words had he been about to speak to her?

How harsh his expression seemed as he watched Ambrose wend his way through the crowded rooms. Why had Lord Bracknell formed so sudden a dislike of Ambrose? For the barest moment she wondered if Bracknell meant to call her cousin out, but this seemed unlikely since the man's only crime had been to evince a desire—however incredible—to speak privately with his own wife, hardly a matter for the dueling field. Yet, as she noted the cool gaze of the man next to her, she had the impression Lord Bracknell meant to bury her cousin, but why?

Chapter Nine

THE MIST SWIRLED about Ambrose as he strolled, cane in hand, toward his rooms in Brook Street. Lamplight in hazy, dim patches kept him going in the right direction, but he had walked this way so frequently that even blindfolded he felt certain he could crawl to his rooms if he had to.

The evening had been most illuminating. His wife, he discovered, was quite serious about that ridiculous Andover fellow. He stabbed the flags with the end of his cane, the echoes of the sound muffled by the fog. He didn't like Jeremy Andover; he never had. But then, he liked so few people nowadays. There were so few who had his sense of taste and refinement, like dear Budgy. Dear, dear Budgy and his endless supply of interesting facts and figures from the war office. Dear, dear Budgy and his short supply of wit.

An odd, muffled whisper reached him, and he stopped in his tracks. It was near dawn and every thief in London was prowling the West End in hopes of an easy prey. And of the moment, since his head was muddled by a second bottle of claret served up at Boodle's not an hour ago, he was precisely that.

He twisted the ivory handle of his cane, and a blade slid smoothly from the handle. Not a moment too soon, for two large cretins rushed at him. He felt the knife meet its mark, and a tall, thin man, his face disguised by a woolen scarf, cursed and fell back. But the other man, a burly, slow fellow, grabbed him securely from behind, pinning his arms, and dragged him into an alleyway near the mews. The smell of horses and sweat nearly made Ambrose retch as fear poured through him. He wanted to shout, to call for help, but for the moment fear had paralyzed him.

The man who had him pinned, spoke in his ear, "The king wants his debts paid, gov. And sooner than later. He's terrible impatient."

The first man who attacked him cried, "He's cut me, the bastard! I'll give him something he'll not forget for a day or two!"

The first blow caught him to the side of his eye, and the dandy cried out, hoping someone passing might hear him and rush to his aid. But a blow to his stomach ended any ability he had to further shout for assistance, and he crumpled to the stones beneath his feet, twisting his ankle. His nose was assailed by vile odors a rivulet of sewage seeping along the street near him.

But all that mattered was that he was still alive, and as the men pilfered his pockets and kicked him for not having had more than three shillings upon his person, he wept with relief that "the king" had let him live. He was late with his payment of interest again, and he was certain word was circulating about the underworld that his wife had taken a lover and that his own sporadic source of funds—his connection to the Warfield estate—was fast dwindling. Even Mrs. Stratfield had nearly refused him entrance to her gaming establishment until he told her he wished only to speak with his wife.

As he sat up, just now able to command his breath, he pressed the wound near his eye. It felt sticky with blood. Afraid he would be sick, he tried not to think of the attack as he staggered to his feet. He was trembling, but his head was amazingly clear. After making certain he would not fall, he limped carefully to the street, where he made his way home as quickly as possible.

To his surprise, Budgy was waiting for him in his rooms. "Thank God you are here, Hazeley. Good heavens! What happened to you?"

Ambrose related the incident to his friend, while holding a kerchief to his head. After finishing the recital of the attack, he said, "I've got to get another loan somewhere until I'm able to get the snuffbox from Ellen. I suppose you've heard Bracknell already has the fan and kerchief?"

Budgy wasted no time, but burst out with "That is what I've come to tell you." He moved wildly about the parlor and once or twice shifted the drapes by the front window and peered into the mist. "I can only stay a moment. If I am found to have visited you, I should be taken to jail immediately. They know about us—they have for some time."

A bout of dizziness washed over Ambrose, his stomach again feeling queasy. "What—what do you mean? They cannot possibly know? Who would've told them?"

Budgy doubled over, his face paling as he dropped into a chair littered with sporting magazines. "I don't know. I only found out because I've a couple of friends who warned me, putting themselves in a terrible fix should their indiscretions become known; I'm grateful to them, beyond words—but I've got to leave."

Budgy wiped his forehead with a cambric pocket handkerchief, and Ambrose could see his hands were shaking.

Rising slowly from his chair, Ambrose limped toward the fireplace and tugged on the bellpull.

Shading his face with his hand, Budgy said, "The fact is, Lord Bracknell's been placed to ferret you out. I—" His pale complexion turned an ashen hue as he doubled over from the waist, his greatcoat still hanging about his shoulders.

"You look like the devil, Budgy."

Budgy nodded, "I haven't had . . . " His voice trailed off.

Ambrose began unbuttoning his own greatcoat. When his sleepy-eyed servant arrived, he handed the coat to him and said, "As you can see, Jaspar, I needed you after all. I'm sorry to have disturbed your slumbers. Please have this cleaned immediately."

Jaspar lifted a brow at the noxious odors emanating

from the coat and held it at a distance from himself, responding with "Very good, sir." He then regarded the cut over his master's eye, his expression one of astonishment, and added, "And perhaps a little sticking plaster?"

Ambrose said, "Yes, and a bottle of Madeira."

The door closed as the servant uttered another "Very good, sir," and Ambrose turned to lift the coat from his friend's shoulder.

"I can't stay," Budgy cried, perspiration again dotting his forehead.

"And you can't leave . . . not until you are feeling a trife better."

After hanging the coat on a stand by the door, Ambrose seated himself across from his friend. He tested his cane several times, to see if it had become damaged in the scuffle, but the blade was intact, with only a small trace of blood smeared on the very tip. He wiped it clean and said, "At least the king's messengers did not walk away entirely unscathed."

Budgy regarded the blade and cried, "What more can go amiss?"

"Just so."

Budgy winced as he pressed a hand to his puffy face, his brown eyes dulled with pain. "Hazeley, I've booked passage next week on a clipper setting sail for the colonies. Come with me. There's nothing left here except Tyburn Tree." He held his stomach, still slightly bent over.

The door opened, and Jaspar brought in the wine, served both men, then carefully applied the sticking plaster to the cut on Ambrose's head. When he had gone, the gentlemen remained silent for a few minutes sipping their wine.

Ambrose stared at the pathetic face of his friend and remembered the way Bracknell had watched him, as though waiting to pounce. At least now he understood why. But he didn't care about that; he wanted the money. There would be money in the transaction regardless that it was a trap. The French were bound to want the coded information, and he wanted the money. He just had to be smarter than all of them.

Budgy said, "They mean to entrap you and the Frenchies with the fan and the other articles. And I've just heard the French are offering fifteen thousand pounds." He gulped the rest of his wine down. "I just want a little peace. But you've been good to me, given me the ready—"

Ambrose cut him off, unable to credit the size of the reward. "Fifteen thousand! Why, that's a fortune! They must believe it is of tremendous value. Are you certain?"

"This scheme has been in motion for over six months, or so I've heard, and great pains have been taken to give an appearance of validity." A carriage rattled down the street, and Budgy cried, "I must leave. I have stayed too long!"

Ambrose stood up and moved to his desk drawer, where he withdrew a small package. With a smile, he turned to face Budgy. "We are a pair, are we not? Here, a little farewell gift, then." And he tossed the package to his friend.

Budgy leaned back in his chair and closed his eyes. He began laughing in a way that irritated Ambrose. "You have saved me, my friend. And what a fine traveling present, a cake of opium." Looking up at Ambrose, he asked, "You mean to have that fortune, don't you?"

Ambrose smiled again but refused to answer.

On the following day Ellen and Celeste sat quietly in the drawing room, Ellen upon the settee of blue brocade and Celeste waiting with drawn features upon an Empire chair with pale lavender stripes. The latter held a small vinaigrette crafted in mother-of-pearl, a gift from Jeremy, and uneasily turned it over and over in her hands.

A carriage clattered in the square Celeste rose quickly and crossed the room to stare down into the street. "It is Ambrose. What are we to do? What am I to tell him? I don't wish to see him—I am afraid to speak with him."

Ellen twisted around to better see her sister, who stood backed by the windows, the morning light framing her in a soft glow. She was dressed in a dove-gray gown and appeared very vulnerable. "You must be firm, dearest, and no matter what he says, you must make it clear you will have nothing to do with him," Ellen told her.

"He can be very persuasive," Celeste said, her voice trailing off as she smoothed the little box in her hand.

"He is a monster. He took your inheritance and caused it to vanish before any of us had time to turn around."

Celeste laughed and recrossed the room to sit beside Ellen. "Yes," she said, "he always was a monster, and I always loved him." She looked at her sister. "How could I love someone who has so completely ruined my life, someone who has not even seen his own children in three years? But now I fear for Jeremy. Oh, what am I to do?"

The doors opened slowly, and the dandy limped into the room, his eye swollen. The ladies gasped.

Bowing slowly as though it afforded him great pain, Ambrose said, "You are both very kind and more than gracious to have permitted me to come here like this."

Celeste, her voice full of pity, cried, "Brosy, what happened to you?"

He placed a hand over his heart and closed his eyes. Ellen thought he appeared as though he might swoon, and when he opened his eyes, they were wet with tears. He said. "How long it has been since I have heard you use that silly, adorable nickname." And gazing steadily at her, he added, "Too long."

Celeste began to protest as did Ellen, but he lifted a hand as though accepting that neither of the ladies wished him to speak such heartfelt words. As he advanced into the room, he explained his condition. "Last night, when I was so distraught—no, I won't burden you further with my sentiments—I decided to walk home. I know it was foolish, but somehow I thought this cane would suffice to protect me from any attack. But I was not prepared for the four ruffians who dragged me into a deserted alleyway and set upon my person."

Ellen felt Celeste's hand creep into her own and knew Celly was asking for help. She said, "Please sit down,

Ambrose, and believe that we are most sorry for your misfortune."

He responded with a sad smile. "It is nothing, truly."

Ellen noticed the way his eyes shifted beneath her steady scrutiny and a vague suspicion took shape in her mind. She did not know what had happened to him, but she thought perhaps it had something to do with his debts and she asked, "Did your creditors, perchance, become tired of waiting?"

She did not mistake the very brief dart of surprise that flashed in her cousin's eyes. She had guessed correctly.

He seemed to suppress a biting retort as he said, "I was robbed."

Celeste started to speak, but Ellen squeezed her hand very hard. She then gestured to the wing chair by the fireplace and begged her cousin to be seated. She could not help but wonder why he had come. Did he truly believe he could win back his wife's affection? As he seated himself gingerly upon the chair, she concluded that he was playing a very deep game and one that involved keeping up the pretense of his connection to Warfield Hall. It was not at all uncommon for tradesmen to begin dunning a client who lost all his future prospects. And Celeste's sudden appearance in London in an estranged living arrangement would undoubtedly have caused a great rift in her cousin's precariously balanced world.

She smiled to herself. What a cunning thief he was. And how easily he could manipulate the feelings of others, though she herself rarely felt anything for him but the strongest revulsion.

Settling into the chair, he said, "I had not wished to be the bearer of ill tidings, but fate has given me no choice." A challenging gleam entered his green-gold eyes as he continued. "I have a very dear friend who holds a minor position in the war office, and he has passed along a most disturbing piece of information—news that affects my family so greatly that *my friend* felt compelled to inform me immediately, even overriding the dangerous and secretive nature of the information. I only wish I could spare you both, but most particularly you, Ellen, from facts that will undoubtedly hurt you. I wish to add I am not unaware that you have recently formed a very strong attachment to a certain gentleman, but I am here to tell you the man in question is an enemy of England."

Celeste and Ellen exchanged looks of considerable astonishment. Ellen had been so certain Ambrose meant to make love to his unhappy wife that she had never imagined he had any other purpose in his visit. And especially not something so very ridiculous.

"An enemy of England?" Ellen asked. "To whom are you referring? You do not mean Lord Bracknell?"

Ambrose crossed his legs, a large bunch of fobs and seals jingling as he did so, and with a satisfied smile, responded, "I refer to none other!"

Chapter Ten

ELLEN LEANED BACK into the brocade settee, her mind and heart reeling under the shock of her cousin's words. Bracknell? An enemy of England? Impossible.

The drawing room misted all around the edges of her vision, time became inordinately slow, and a thin film of perspiration dampened her brow. She had felt this way before, on the day she had sat in her papa's library and listened to the solicitor read parts of the infamous will. And, as last time, her hearing seemed to disappear—she could not hear what Ambrose was saying. How dry her mouth suddenly became, thoughts of Bracknell flittering across her mind like a great flock of birds at nightfall.

Finally Ambrose stopped speaking entirely, and the room grew silent. Only then did some of the disordered thoughts flying about her brain find a resting place. She heard a voice travel from a great distance, a soft feminine voice, "Ellen, Ellen, you are hurting my hand. Dearest, are you all right?"

Ellen turned to view Celeste and after blinking several times, saw her pallid complexion and light blue eyes come sharply into focus. She released the harsh grip she had on her sister's hand and whispered, "It cannot be Hugh. It cannot!"

Celeste began weeping. "We are both accursed!"

Ellen placed an arm about her shoulder and patted her gently. Only then did she see the faint smile of satisfaction upon her cousin's face, and she realized something about Ambrose—he was filled with hate. And wouldn't such a person, a care-for-nobody, a gamester, enjoy telling lies, just to hurt, just to enjoy seeing someone else suffer? Or was it possible he knew of her father's will and was trying to prevent a marriage he had suddenly come to believe was a distinct possibility?

A small dart of hope pierced her breast, and she set about calming Celeste and at the same time tried to think of just how she might entrap Ambrose into an admission of his knowledge.

Celeste began muttering about the horrid will and about gamesters in general, and Ellen grew afraid her sister would reveal the truth about the conditions of the will if she were allowed to continue indulging her sensibilities. She ordered Celeste to blow her nose, repeatedly telling her to hush, and when she wouldn't Ellen finally resorted to pinching her just above the elbow.

Celeste gave a cry and pulled away from her sister. When she realized what Ellen was trying so desperately to communicate to her, she burst into a truly noisy bout of fabricated tears.

Ellen let out a sigh of relief and turned her attention to the task of forming just the right question for Ambrose.

Finally, as Celeste allowed her sobs to subside, Ellen asked her cousin, "I gather, then, that you know of my father's will?"

He lifted a brow, a faint look of surprise crossing his features. He said, "No, I do not."

Ellen studied him carefully. "Yes, the estate is forfeit to the British Museum if I do not marry within the week. I had hoped to wed Lord Bracknell."

A flush broke out in very strange blotches all over the dandy's face, and he rose to his feet abruptly. Placing a hand at his temple, above his blackened eye, he cried in disgust, "The British Museum! Of all the beetle-brained—" He broke off suddenly, realizing he had just erred.

But Ellen heard his ingenuous cry and knew he did not have a clue as to the true nature of the will. Part of her was relieved, for she had the strongest impression were he to know of the will, he would do everything in his power, short of murder—and even then, she wondered—to gain the estate.

A shudder went through her as Ambrose met her gaze, his own eyes narrowed. Every hint of his former concern disappeared entirely as he cried, "What nonsense is this? The British Museum, indeed!"

Celeste shrank back into the settee and drew in her breath sharply. "He is unchanged," she whispered. "He shifts from light to dark as quickly as the snuffing of a candle. I have always been a fool. I have always seen what I have wanted to see."

Ellen heard Celeste's voice and felt sorry for her, now that her disillusionment in her husband was complete. But if Ambrose knew nothing of the will, then what he was saying of Bracknell might possibly be true. She returned her glance to her cousin, who had reseated himself in the wing chair and was now swinging one leg over the other. His expression, as he lifted his quizzing glass and peered at her, was one of intense dislike. For whatever reasons, he had given up all pretense. His smiles were completely gone.

In a flat voice, he said, "I don't know what reason you had for shamming it, Ellen, but it won't fadge. Playing deep, are you?"

Ellen nodded slowly. "As it happens, I am. My father did leave a condition to his will, but I won't tell you what it is."

He fairly squinted at her, his green-gold eyes narrowing as he tried to guess. "I can tell you right now I know it has to do with Bracknell. You've been humbugged, m'dear. Tell me, does he have possession of your telegraph fan, a gold-embroidered kerchief, and that intricate gold snuffbox of your father's? French spies operating in Portsmouth are waiting even now for Bracknell to arrive with the articles in hand, and they have offered a considerable fortune—fifteen thousand pounds."

Ellen drew in a sharp breath. Fifteen thousand? Enough

to settle anyone's debts or even to pay off a mortgage. It could not be true; it could not! These were her father's gifts to her.

She answered slowly, "Bracknell has my fan, but not the snuffbox . . ." Here she paused and regarded her hands, which were tightly clenched upon her lap. She tried to relax them, but they refused, her arms aching up to her shoulders. "And he has possessed my kerchief for nearly three weeks now."

Ambrose smiled at her in an extremely smug fashion as he twirled his quizzing glass on its silk riband.

Ellen shook her head in disbelief. Impossible, she thought. Bracknell wouldn't; he couldn't. He might be a gamester, he might have mortgaged Three Elms, but never could she believe his character so bad that he would actually resort to betraying his country. Yet she could not deny the many times she had felt uneasy with Lord Bracknell, as though something were not quite right, particularly when giving him the kerchief and the fan.

As she sat staring at her whitening knuckles, the most horrifying revelation of all descended upon her—she loved him; she loved a spy.

A spy. Impossible! She lifted her chin, her fingers now clutching her morning gown of pink muslin. "I don't believe you."

Ambrose threw his head back and laughed, the quizzing glass falling to rest upon his yellow-striped waistcoat. "The golden heiress, having fallen violently in love with a traitor to England, now lies shattered at the base of her own pedestal. How curious. How tragic. My poor cousin!"

Ellen was about to defend herself hotly when Celeste's voice intruded, "I don't believe you either, Mr. Hazeley. How could either of us believe a man who is as given to gaming and lying as you. I used to pity my sons because they never saw their father, and now I am glad. I despise you, Ambrose Hazeley, and I wish you to the devil."

"My, my," he said in a honeyed tone, "so, the little mouse has a voice and has taken to cursing. I only wish you had shown such spirit when we were first married; I might not have strayed as I did."

"You are not fit to breathe the same air as Lord Bracknell," Celeste cried. "I know him for what he is, a very fine, honorable gentleman. How dare you mince in here and cast such damaging aspersions on the man Ellen hopes to make her husband."

Ambrose had been listening to his wife, but at this final statement he turned toward Ellen and said, "So all of it is true! You hope to make him your husband. I had heard such gossip in the clubs, but I wasn't certain. Of course you are terribly smitten, so I am not in the least surprised. But, tell me, are you also selling our secrets to the French?"

Ellen stared at her cousin. She hated him, and his words drove her to her feet. "You scoundrel, you cur! I only wish the ruffians who attacked you had also torn out your heart. But would they have found such an organ buried in your chest?" She flung an arm toward him, gesturing wildly. "How greatly I doubt it, you scurrilous knave!"

Ambrose relaxed even further into his chair, his cheek now propped up with his hand, one long, thin leg still slung over the other and rocking in a contented fashion. "A veritable Siddons! Pray, continue. I am vastly entertained."

This reference to one of England's finest actresses did little to allay Ellen's hot temper, and she strode to the window, trying to calm herself.

Ambrose pressed a pained hand against his chest as he continued, "You may think whatever you like, but the facts must speak for themselves. All of London knows he is nearly rolled up—he needs the funds, unless of course he marries you, Ellen, and then I suppose he could replenish his bank account and his estates at liberty." This thought seemed to give him great pleasure in some odd fashion, and he peered up at the ceiling and mused, "Perhaps I could even suggest to him that he ask for your hand. A little word, gently placed in his ear: 'Marry the golden heiress; forget the Frenchies.' Faith, the more I consider the matter, the less I credit the man with any sense at all."

He rose to his feet. "Believe what you will. I am an imperfect being, but I meant only good to come of this tête-à-tête. I should dislike immensely to have such a scandal besmirch our precious family name."

"Beast," Celeste said through clenched teeth.

He bowed to his wife and said sweetly, "Good day, my love."

Ellen turned to face him. "You are no longer welcome in this house. Pray leave and never return."

"How blind your love has made you." He sighed deeply. "But consider this: all could be settled if you would but offer the snuffbox to him. If he took it, you would know the truth. And you would know it by the measuring glance in his eye as he debated whether or not to take it from you. I know precisely how he would look: he would salivate."

Ellen watched him straighten his white-satin coat, then limp with head held high toward the door. When his footsteps disappeared down the stairwell, Ellen took a deep breath, feeling as though she might faint. Dropping onto a hard-backed chair by the window, she pressed a hand to her forehead, closing her eyes. "No, it cannot be," she whispered.

She heard Celeste approach and felt her sister place an arm about her shoulders. "Ambrose is a liar! I tell you he is. Bracknell is no more a traitor than I am. You must trust me in this. I did not live with my husband for so long a time without coming to comprehend his character a little."

Ellen opened her eyes and studied her sister. She met pale blue eyes full of concern, and she reached up to press her sister's arm very hard. "I don't know what to make of it. You do not know all. At Mrs. Stratfield's, after we had done playing hazard, we moved to a roulette table where Bracknell wagered for the very snuffbox Ambrose was referring to. Oh, how ill I feel suddenly."

Celeste shook her head in disbelief, "Are you certain it was the same one?"

"Why would he ask for one of father's snuffboxes at all? It doesn't make sense, unless—oh, I cannot think of it! My heart is breaking."

Turning to stare down into the street, Celeste frowned and said, "He is just leaving. I never thought I could despise him as much as I do. And worse, if you do not marry Bracknell—spy or no—that detestable man," and she pointed an accusing finger toward the street, "will inherit Warfield Hall."

Ellen, however, did not entirely agree with her sister. There was one thing worse than Ambrose inheriting the hall—that she had lost her heart not only to a gamester and a libertine, but to a traitor as well.

As Ellen slowly released her sister's arm, she knew her cousin had suggested the only thing she could do in this situation. She must discover the truth, and she could only do that by offering the snuffbox to Lord Bracknell. With that thought, she succumbed to a hearty bout of tears.

Once she had composed herself, Ellen retired to the quiet of her own bedchamber to consider carefully what she would need to do. She sat in a chair by the window and watched the gray skies above the metropolis grow black and heavy, rain finally burtsing onto her windowpane in a loud, angry frenzy.

The rain reflected her mood completely, and she wished she could release all her frustration and hurt by beating upon something. But even as she considered rending her pillow to pieces as she had when she was younger and did not get her way, the very idea struck her as not only completely unsatisfactory, but childish as well. And spoiled, just as her papa had stated in his letter.

She knew nothing could possibly relieve her distress at even the notion of Lord Bracknell as a traitor. Traitor—never was a word more vile than that! And she had fallen in love with him! Oh, why had her father forced this upon her with his stupid will? She had always believed her papa so clever and wise. But this? Had he never suspected Lord Bracknell? She knew her father had been acquainted with the viscount and also that he had often been in company with the Duke of York and very frequently the Prince Regent. The possibilities of such connections tumbled across Ellen's mind in a rapid fire of pain.

She realized suddenly that Bracknell, through his friendship with her father, could easily have discovered bits of information worthy of sale to French agents. Her heart felt deeply burdened as she mulled the matter over in her mind and saw what Ambrose had seen—that Bracknell had every reason, as a gamester who had mortgaged his own estates, and every possibility, as a friend to persons of authority, to execute whatever nefarious schemes he wished.

She rested her forehead against the cold windowpane, the glass soothing her burning skin. Her father had brought this all down upon her head with the conditions of his will. But in this she could not fault him entirely. He had not told her to lose her heart to Bracknell. He had not said she should suffer or unwittingly fall in love with a traitor. He had said only to make him her husband.

With that thought she sat bolt upright in the chair. A plan took sudden and startling shape in her brain. She must make him her husband. Her predicament was as simple as that. Traitor or no, her task was clearly before her—she must marry him; she must preserve her inheritance.

A measure of relief began to flow through her as thunder echoed across Mayfair. She looked out upon the brick buildings across the square at the rain lashing in torrents. A hackney pulled before the town house, and Ellen was a little startled to see Celeste run from the house toward the coach. Jeremy leapt from the hackney, rain pelting his beaver hat, and caught her in his arms. Celeste spoke urgently to him, and then he kissed her very hard on the mouth. Ellen turned away, feeling slightly numb, for it was clear something had just been decided between them. What more could go awry? She would speak with Celeste immediately. Her sister could not be planning another elopement! Indeed, she could not.

She rose to her feet and shook out the skirts of her pink muslin gown as though preparing to do battle. She had meant to repair at once to her sister's bedchamber and await her there, but a scratching at the bedchamber door arrested her progress.

Becky peeked her head around the edge of the door, then emerged fully into the room wearing a bright smile. "Have you rested a bit, then?" she asked. "I have a letter for you and would have brought it up sooner, but you seemed as though you wished to be quiet for a little while."

She crossed the room to Ellen and handed her a large packet of thick paper tied with a red silk ribbon. It was from Mr. Ibthorpe. What now? "What more can my father's solicitor have to tell me?" she whispered into the air.

Becky moved to the fireplace and began stirring the coals. She looked back over her shoulder and said, "Well, don't just stand there, miss, looking like it's a thing from beyond the grave. Open it up. No doubt, it's not so bad as you think."

To the sound of the poker scraping across the hearth, Ellen untied the ribbon and read Mr. Ibthorpe's very short note informing her her father had wanted her to have the enclosed document on day twenty-three following the reading of the will.

She set aside the solicitor's letter, and though she read the document carefully, it took her several minutes before she realized she was staring at a special license.

"A special license?" she cried. The document, with its obvious implications, set fire to a temper that had been smoldering for weeks, and all her previous serenity deserted her. "Why . . . why . . . how dare he! I don't care if he is dead. He is a meddling old fool, and I hate him for this. I shall never forgive him for forcing me to wed a gamester and a traitor and . . . and everything I despise!"

She was so furious, she crumpled the license up and threw it toward the fireplace. Fortunately it banked off Becky's hip and fell harmlessly to the carpeted floor.

After a shriek of sheer frustration, Ellen threw herself onto the bed. She buried her face in the pillow and screamed until her voice had disappeared into a ragged cough. The fit passed, and she wondered for a moment if she would ever feel sane again.

When she had quieted, she rolled on her side and found herself staring into the face of a Becky she did not recognize. She was frightened at the expression on her maid's face and sat up quickly, as though she were a little girl and had just been caught in some reprehensible mischief. Her slippered feet, sporting large yellow-satin bows, dangled over the edge of the bed, completing a picture of youth and guilt.

Becky placed both hands on her wide hips and scowled at her mistress. "Now, I've had just about enough of your little baby freaks. Mr. Warfield must have spoiled you uncommonly bad to have had his daughter, *his* daughter! turn out so ill-tempered and peabrained." Her face turned an alarming shade of red, and all her freckles appeared to merge together.

Ellen stared hard at her maid, her defenses leaping into position as she heard this quite improper tirade burst from Becky's lips. Becky was her servant and had no right to be speaking to her in this completely high-handed fashion. She felt her chin jut out mulishly and defiantly, and in a small angry voice that sounded horribly childish to her own ears, she protested, "How dare you take that tone with me, Becky Lovedean!"

"And who's to stop me!" Becky cried. "You ought to go about the world a little more, Miss High and Mighty, and see what real suffering is like. You have a staff of fifteen here to wait on you—and thirty at the hall—to pick up your clothes, to see that your chamber pot is emptied, and to put a warming pan in your bed at night. Oh, I feel that sorry for you, I do." She threw her arms out theatrically, then drew them back onto her ample bosom. "Oh, my heart bleeds, it does. Poor Miss Warfield, has to marry the handsomest, finest man I've ever known, has to do her papa's bidding and she don't like it. La, how cruel fate is to some of us. Well, let me tell you, Miss Priss, you ain't worth half the likes of Bracknell, and I pity him if he ever does agree to become your husband, for a nastier shrew I've never known. And if you ain't got the sense to figure out what's going on beneath your own short, stubby little nose, then I say you deserve everything you get."

Ellen reached up and felt the tip of her nose. It was a

stupid thing to have done and only made her feel even more like an errant child. She was about to speak, but Becky cut her off.

"And you've as much sense as a donkey I had as a pet once when I was little. Nay, that's being unkind to the poor animal's memory. You've got the sense of a dungcock." And on this last note, the maid shook her apron out, tweaked the curls on her forehead with hastily moistened fingers, and stomped out.

"Becky," Ellen wailed.

The silence in Ellen's bedchamber hurt her ears. She felt utterly and completely humiliated. The sound of Celeste's voice down the hallway only made the accusing quiet of her room even more penetrating. Over the last three weeks she had heard the same relentless theme of her stubbornness and her childish ways recurring again and again, like the constant tapping of the rain against the windows.

She remained sitting on the edge of her bed and stared down at the bows of her slippers. A little girl, a spoiled little girl, facing the first crisis of her life—whatever the cause—and all she could do was indulge in a bout of tears and throw fits upon her bed. Was she so very bad? Becky seemed to think so, as did her papa.

She reached down to her feet and slowly removed each of her slippers, cradling them on her lap. These were old slippers of hers. Very old. Old-fashioned, in fact, for her mother had made the little satin bows for her just before she died.

A tear fell from her eye and splashed onto one of the soft shoes. How lost and uncertain she felt. Never had she felt the lack of a mother so acutely as now. There had been no one to guide her in all these years. She had taken to managing Warfield Hall shortly after her mother's death and had reveled in it, fitting neatly into her mama's shoes, walking beside the housekeeper and inspecting all the rooms, directing the gardener's efforts in planting the spring flower beds, calling upon the sick and the poor. Somehow it had lessened her grief.

Only now did picking up her mother's duties feel like a

terrible weight to her, a grief even, as though a little part of her had been locked up in childhood and not allowed to grow up properly. The womanly part of her. Her heart ached with feelings she did not even understand, and she pressed the slippers to her breast as she called her mother's name softly in the quiet chamber.

Early Monday morning, just before the night turned to a coal gray as the sun invaded the evening's debaucheries, Becky pulled her cape close about her neck and rapped on the door to Ambrose Hazeley's small town house. His manservant, hastily dressed to answer Becky's repeated raps of the brass knocker, intended to turn the hooded female away, until he saw who it was. And then his ferocious scowl—for he was prepared to do battle with the nervy wench if necessary—turned into a lascivious grin and he cried, "Becky! My little turtledove."

He pulled her by the arm, drawing her roughly into the ill-lit entrance hall, where he took her immediately in his arms.

Becky was quite pleased with this very masculine response to her presence and would have gladly obliged him by returning his ardor but she had serious matters to attend to. Pressing her hands against his chest, she spoke in a firm voice, "No, Jaspar, I've not the time. I must speak with your master. It's frightfully urgent."

But Jaspar, consumed with a sudden passion, gripped her more fiercely still, so that Becky found it necessary to crunch the heel of her half boot down firmly upon his instep. He cried out, and the sudden stirrings from the bedchamber abovestairs caused the servant to curse softly and push Becky hastily into the front parlor while he hurried to close the front door. The rush of wind this occasioned nearly extinguished the lone candle that dimly illuminated the small entrance hall. When her beau returned to the parlor door, Becky could not resist laughing at his funny appearance as he tried to straighten a waistcoat that was improperly buttoned and ballooned out about mid-chest.

Becky could not see the entrance hall, but she could

hear Ambrose descend the stairs. Jaspar's shoulders were now laid back as though he were about to salute a commanding officer.

She heard Ambrose call to him, "What is it? What is going on?"

Without blinking, Jaspar announced Becky. "A female person to see you, Mr. Hazeley. I told her it was very late, but she insisted it was a matter of some import."

Ambrose approached the doorway, the blade unsheathed from his cane, and peered in. His eyes were wide and dilated. "Who is it?" he demanded.

"You are not acquainted with me, Mr. Hazeley. My name is Becky Lovedean, and I am Miss Ellen's personal maid. I have grave matters to discuss with you."

Returning the blade to its hidden sheath, Ambrose entered the room and dismissed his servant with a wave of his hand. Becky regarded Jaspar's frantic hand motions as he faced the room for just a moment before he disappeared down the hallway. She felt a sudden desire to seek out the servant as soon as she had completed her mission with Celeste's husband. Jaspar had a way of kissing that curled her toes.

She turned her attention to Ambrose and felt repulsed by the sight of his thin, almost emaciated frame covered only by yellow inexpressibles, a linen shirt, and frayed Moroccan slippers.

He regarded her with a considering expression. "Your face did seem rather familiar, but isn't this an odd hour for a young woman to be walking about these inadequately guarded streets alone and unprotected?"

"I'm quite familiar with the streets, sir. I've lived in London for nearly fifteen years, even in those miserable parts at t'other end. I know how to make certain of my safety—I always hire a large, healthy hackney driver." She wondered how he had gotten the bruise above his eye.

Ambrose did not hesitate to walk to the front window, limping slightly from his misadventure of the night before. Peering out into the misty morning, he saw the burly, slumped form of the driver and said, "A clever wench, eh?"

"I am that," she answered evenly. "Which is why I've come to you. I have information I think you will find not only of considerable use, but entertaining as well. And I'll gladly impart it—for a small fee, of course."

Still holding his cane in hand, he looked back at her and said, "Entertaining?" He lifted a brow. Without taking his gaze from her he crossed the small chamber and set the cane against the fireplace. Only two or three faint red spots glowed dully where the coals had not been completely extinguished. He finally let his eyes shift from her and continued, "I'm afraid, however, that you've mistaken your man, or at least my pocketbook. I've not a feather to fly with."

"I know that. My mistress has complained loudly about you for over a year. But I know something that would be worth a considerable fortune to you, and all I am asking for is a just portion—after the deed is done, that is."

He laughed. "A small fee, eh?" He was not even wearing stockings to ward off the chill of the early-morning hours, so he stayed close to the fireplace and rocked on his heels. Narrowing his eyes at her, he continued, "Either you're telling the truth or you're as mad as bedlam. A considerable fortune, indeed! Does Ellen know you are here? Did she send you with this Canterbury tale to torture me?"

"Ellen Warfield is the worst female I have ever worked for. You know what she is, spoiled and nasty-tempered. I've had nothing but grief from her. And she who has so much and never sharing with those in need! You know what she is, don't you, selfish and greedy!"

Becky watched the line of his jaw harden, emotions working within the dandy that confirmed her assessment of his character. She was not surprised when he said, "She should never have inherited the hall. I was the next male heir. It should have come to me. Vincent could have changed the will; instead he let Ellen inherit that vast estate. It should have been mine. And what sort of man would give a woman precedence over a man?"

"I knew Warfield. I always thought he had a screw loose. I never liked him above half."

Ambrose smiled faintly. "We seem to have a great deal in common."

Becky had not been certain how the interview would proceed, but his smile pleased her very much, and she moved to stand near his desk, where she could see a jumble of tradesmen's bills stuffed carelessly into the center drawer. She said, "What I have to tell you could make you a very wealthy man. It could gain you the estate."

"Now, what maggoty ideas are you brewing in your stewpot, I wonder. Murder, perhaps?"

Becky laughed. "No, something so simple, though, that I daresay you wouldn't credit it. That's why I'm here. I've been waiting for just this sort of opportunity all my life, and here it is. You don't know what it is to be born in squalor, to grow up on gin instead of milk. But I do. And now my time's come and I mean to make full use of it. There's only one thing I'm not certain of—whether you'll hand over the dibs when all's said and done. And there's only four of us that know the facts—me, Miss Ellen, Miss Celeste, and Mr. Ibthorpe."

"Ibthorpe?" Ambrose spoke sharply.

Becky nodded as she sat down in a hard-backed chair near the desk and pushed her hood back. "Warfield's solicitor."

Ambrose scanned the carpet at his feet. It lay slightly askew on the tile floor in front of the hearth, and without thinking too much about it, he put his foot forward and straightened it. Whistling softly through his teeth, he said, "The will."

"You've the right of it."

He looked up at her, his expression quite intense. "There's a condition to her inheritance, isn't there?"

"La, but ain't you a downy one! Have you guessed, then?"

"What is it?"

"Ah, but that's the trick. If I tell you, you'll have no need to pay me."

"I may be many things, Miss Lovedean, but I honor my debts, even if belatedly. You can trust me."

She answered sarcastically, "Oh, I'm sure I can, and this morning the sun will refuse to rise!"

He laughed. "I like you. Indeed, I do."

"I won't return the compliment. I'll only tell you there is one thing you can do. Write out a promise I may have the emerald ring Miss Ellen wears should you come into the property. It's an heirloom; it belongs to the estate. When you're legally the heir, I'll simply take it from her and disappear. And you'll not send anyone after me."

Ambrose did not hesitate. What was one paltry ring in the face of Ellen's fortune? He sat down at his desk and after scuffling about in the drawers for a moment, found a blank sheet of paper. He scribbled Becky's request out in a large, flowery scrawl, dusted the paper with a fine layer of sand, and handed it to her.

Becky was so pleased as she took the paper and read it carefully that she could not refrain from smiling. He was a great deal more gullible than even she suspected, falling neatly into their trap. Vincent had said he would, but she hadn't believed him.

He caught her wrist. "Where did you learn to read?"

How harsh his hand was on her wrist, and she felt her cheeks burn. Perhaps he was smarter than she thought, but she had been well-trained, and the words flowed easily from her lips, "My grandma was a parson's daughter. She taught me."

"You're lying. You've lied about everything. That humbug about gin instead of milk. Who are you?"

Becky tried to jerk her arm free, but he twisted it painfully. "I don't know what you mean. I only want a chance at a real life. I'm taking the ring and going to New South Wales."

"And why would someone connected to a parson have grown up on gin and know how to read?"

"My mother were born on the wrong side of the blanket,

that's all. I only found grandma when I was a girl of thirteen and my mother died. I sought her out. She took care of me for two years before she died. She taught me to read. I swear it on her grave!"

He released her wrist. "If I find out you've gammoned me, Miss Lovedean, I'll slit your throat."

Becky regarded his menacing expression, the green-gold eyes flecked with flashes of angry light, and she had little difficulty believing he would do just that. Swallowing her fear, she said, "If Miss Ellen don't marry Lord Bracknell by this Sunday, she loses everything."

He laughed scornfully. "To the British Museum, no doubt?"

Becky measured her words. "No. To you. I read the will myself. Warfield thought his daughter would grow into a spinster and he'd always liked Bracknell. He decided to force her hand."

Ambrose dropped the quill, still full of ink, onto his yellow breeches and cried, "Good God!"

Becky seated herself carefully in the hackney and allowed Jaspar one last kiss before she drove off. Her heart beat erratically. Events were fast drawing to a close, and as the hackney pulled into the early-morning mist she glanced back to the town house only to find Ambrose staring down at her with a hard expression on his face. She shuddered as she sank back into the seat, pulling her hooded cape more closely about her shoulders. Did Vincent really know what he was doing?

Chapter Eleven

ELLEN FELT JUST as she had more than three weeks earlier when she had sat in Lord Bracknell's library and waited for him to appear. Only this time, it was her own morning room, and the viscount would be arriving at eleven, in a mere five minutes. Her thoughts were so different now, as though the last few weeks hadn't been weeks at all, but years. She felt older, quieter, yet still deeply troubled. She had had so little experience with difficulties of any sort, beyond the impersonal management of the estate, that she found it nearly impossible to sort through all that was happening to her. And now she must face the man she loved and discover whether or not he was a traitor.

She sat quietly on the Egyptian lounge, her arm draped over the side of the couch, her other arm cradling a small package wrapped with a piece of black silk ribbon—grieving ribbon, for she had worn it in her hair for the first month after her father's death. She felt a little dead inside even now, knowing if Bracknell proved a traitor indeed, then she would suffer a similar loss. For though she had determined she must marry him to secure her inheritance, afterward she must turn him over to the London authorities. And what would follow then, but his death by hanging?

She wished more than anything that she was wrong, that Ambrose and his connection at the war office had somehow been mistaken. But every piece of evidence pointed toward Bracknell's guilt.

She loved her country, and all night she had lain awake thinking of the terrible crime he had committed in selling his country's secrets and of the number of lives his greed most certainly had cost England.

But she wouldn't think of that now. She must concentrate instead upon determining the nature of his reaction to her gift, permitting him the measure of justice he deserved as a free Englishman. That must be the focus of her every word, her every thought.

She heard the sound of voices in the hall, followed by footsteps. The door opened, and Lord Bracknell walked in.

The room was fairly large, with white-molded scroll-work trailing over the ceiling. Coals burned white in the fireplace, and the morning mist cloaked the windows in a gray shroud. Even the patterned carpet of purples and reds was dull in the weak, cloudy light, and did little to allay a rather cold appearance to the square chamber. No flowers adorned the dining table, only a large, cold silver epergne.

Ellen did not rise to her feet as Lord Bracknell bowed to her, the package strangely heavy on her lap. As she lifted her gaze to regard him, she watched the habitual gleam of amusement fall away from his face. He had been smiling when he walked in, and now he looked almost horrified. She wondered what he had seen in her own face to cause such a strong shift in his expression. She still leaned on the arm of the couch and heard herself saying good morning and begging him to be seated, but he remained by the door, a frown creasing his brow.

How handsome he looks, she thought in an oddly detached fashion. He was dressed with his usual grace and perfection, a coat of blue superfine, a white neckcloth in careful folds, buff breeches, and an emerald signet ring gleaming on his hand. She smiled at that. She had never known him to exhibit a preference for emeralds. She glanced at his face and saw his frown had lightened a trifle.

His voice was very rich, filling the chamber. "You are

not well. You smiled just then, but I can see you are troubled."

She did not want his sympathy. Her throat constricted all of its own accord, and she was dismayed to realize how close to tears she was. Pressing a hand against her throat, she rubbed her ring against her skin. It felt very cool. She took a deep breath and said, "No, I am not entirely well, my lord. I have the headache a little, but I am grateful to you for attending me this morning. You are very good."

He laughed. "Oh, yes. I am very good."

She glanced sharply at him and frowned.

He finally stepped into the room and advanced toward her, his face taking on something of an irritated aspect. And this time when he spoke he sounded angry. "What is it? What have I done? I can see you are displeased with something, but what, I cannot imagine."

Ellen wanted to blurt out the whole. She wanted to accuse him of being a traitor, of his every past sin, and especially of all Ambrose had told her. And more. She wanted him to tell her it was all a terrible lie, that he hadn't mortgaged Three Elms, that he never gambled, that he loved her! What a wretched morass of thoughts. She pressed a hand to her head.

Lord Bracknell watched Ellen and did not know what to make of her mood. She seemed in pain; she seemed very, very sad. He did not wait for an invitation, but sat down next to her and possessed himself of her hand. Only then did he realize she held a small parcel bound by a black ribbon on her lap. An odd color ribbon for a gift—if it was a gift.

Then he understood it all. He knew what was in the package—Vincent's snuffbox. And that could only mean Ellen knew, but knew what? Who would have told her?

He held her hand tightly, fear striking his heart. Ambrose had told her something, but what had he told her? Now she had indeed become a pawn, played by both sides against the middle. How much should he now reveal to her? Would the truth jeopardize Vincent's original plan?

Would Ellen be put in even greater danger if she knew the truth?

He placed an arm about her shoulders and in a quiet voice, said, "Ellen, tell me what has happened. Please, you may trust me."

She looked into concerned hazel eyes, her heart aching, and said, "Can I, my lord?"

He was too near her, too close to her golden hair, which inevitably had that strange effect upon him, making him want to bury his face in its glossy depths. What a silly reaction. He felt the most ridiculous chub. But he loved her hair. He loved her. Good God, he loved her!

And why had he not seen it before? And when had it begun? Perhaps years ago, when she stood on the terrace of Warfield Hall, summer shining in her face. The revelation of his love sent a fire through him and whatever her mood, whatever her sentiments toward him, he could not resist turning her abruptly toward him and taking her fiercely in his arms. And he did not hesitate to say, "I love you, Ellen. I think I have for these ten years and more." She seemed deeply shocked as he looked into her startling green eyes, her face first appearing stricken, then overcome with a light so radiant that he waited for no gentle permission but drew her into a feverish embrace.

Ellen lost herself in his love. She stood on the very brink of a tall cliff and gently gave herself to a warm breeze that gathered her up and carried her out into a sky of the calmest, sweetest blue. His love eased the worries from her heart, and she felt free to glide higher and higher, the breeze twisting her around and around until she was so wonderfully dizzy that laughter bubbled from deep within her. She pulled away from him, a joy so great overtaking her that she could not stop from laughing, and when she opened her eyes, she realized she was standing upright, held fast in his arms, her feet resting securely upon his polished Hessians.

He had been whirling her around in a circle, and she

hadn't even been completely aware of it—just lost in the joy of his love.

"Hugh," she cried. "I love you!"

He kissed her again, holding her so hard she could scarcely breathe. She did not want this moment to end, and she threw her arms about his neck and pressed herself into him, wishing she could melt her body into his and never leave him again. Never. Oh, how she loved him!

The fierceness receded; the kisses became very sweet, and gentle words flowed over her cheeks, caressing her ears and traveling in a warm rivulet to her heart, easing all the pain of too many years past counting. She leaned against him, nestling her head against his shoulder, holding him fast, letting tears flow gently down her cheeks.

Only then did she see the package, now crumpled on the floor, the ribbon untied and part of the gold snuffbox peeking through. She felt so ill in that moment, she nearly fainted. "No, no, no," she whispered softly, holding him even more tightly. "It cannot be true. It cannot. I cannot love a . . . "

Lord Bracknell tried to pull her away from his shoulder, but Ellen clung to him. If he let her go, she would have to ask for the truth, and she didn't want to. If she pulled away, she would lose him forever.

Finally, as he struggled with her, he spoke sharply, "Enough, Ellen. What is it?"

She jerked away from him and wiped an angry tear from her cheek. She reached down, retrieved the package, and thrust it toward him. "This is what is the matter!" And she turned away from him, folding her arms across her chest as though in doing so she could keep her heart from breaking.

Bracknell unwrapped the rest of the paper, letting the ribbon fall to the floor. Within the package was a gold snuffbox and two little yellow bows. Whatever did she mean by the bows, and what did she know of Vincent's plans?

"I don't understand?"

"You said you wanted the snuffbox and . . . and I wish you to have it. In . . . in memory of my father."

"And what are these?"

Ellen glanced over her shoulder, saw the little yellow bows, and immediately averted her gaze. "They are my innocence, Hugh." Taking a deep breath, her voice quiet, she continued, "And now tell me why you wanted Papa's snuffbox."

Lord Bracknell knew his love was suffering from an emotion so great, she was nearly curling up into a little ball right in front of him. But what disturbed him more was that she refused to trust him.

He remained silent for a moment, and when he finally spoke, his voice was considerably subdued. "You seem to be laboring under some strong emotion I do not understand. What you have surmised about my desire to possess your father's snuffbox, I can only guess." He meant to tell her something of her father's plans, to give her a hint at the dastardly business involving her cousin so nearly, but suddenly he felt very angry and hurt. Did she suppose he meant to sell the objects to the French himself?

A brilliant light flashed through his mind, and he knew that was precisely what Ambrose had told her. Of course. He realized, too, she had every reason to believe him so bad—hadn't he made a spectacle of himself in the clubs about the West End? Hadn't it carefully been put about that he had mortgaged Three Elms? Didn't he in fact give all the appearance of a hardened gamester, one on the brink of ruin—like Hazeley—who might resort to traitorous schemes in order to restore his fortunes?

Still, a little part of him cried out to her, begging for her trust. He noted her hunched shoulders, and a terrible amusement stole over him, a mischievous feeling that often overtook him when he faced a difficult situation. Life seemed to hold so many ridiculous ironies, and they always caused such tremendous pain that there was nothing really to do but laugh and get over the rough ground as lightly as possible.

This he decided to do. Rather than try to force her hand, to expect her to trust him blindly, he walked forward and slipped his arms about her. Oh, but he was bad, very bad to be doing this. But she deserved it, the minx, for not believing in him but a little. And if that weren't enough to justify the truly wretched thing he was about to do, he rationalized that for the next few days all would be better if Ellen were safely out of the picture.

He cradled her gently and felt her hand grip his arm in a desperate fashion. "My sweet peagoose. You must trust me." Oh, he was so very bad. "I have a scheme going now that will eradicate every debt of mine entirely." He squeezed her very hard. "But I must leave town for a few days and will return in time to marry you before the conditions of your father's will have expired, so you may rest easy on that head. And just think how very rich I—that is, we shall be." He sighed gustily, having said enough to cause even a saint to doubt him forever.

Ellen's hurt and betrayal metamorphosed to a white-hot anger so quickly, engulfing her so completely, that she felt her head would simply fly off if she did not do something. Whirling out of his arms, she struggled with emotions so violent, she could only stand staring at him, her breast heaving with rage.

She wanted to stamp her foot—but she remembered her father's accusations. She wanted to throw a truly nasty fit, but she remembered Becky's horrible lecture. She wanted to throw a very heavy object at him, but she glanced at the bows he still held in his hand, and the edge to her ire dissipated.

It was time to leave her girlhood behind.

Swallowing hard, she straightened her shoulders, and held her hands tightly together. "Pray leave, Lord Bracknell. You and I can have nothing to say to each other. And please do not return to . . . to wed me. I had rather be impoverished forever than marry such a man as you." And on that note, she lifted a dramatic arm, pointing him toward the door.

He did not move for a moment, and Ellen lifted her brows in an inquiring, haughty fashion. He smiled with a gentle expression on his face, one that cut through her heart again, as he said, "You are infinitely adorable, and I will return to marry you. I shan't give you a choice about that: the matter is fully decided."

He left her trembling and uncertain. When he closed the door behind him, she felt as though the gates of heaven had just as firmly shut her out. As always, she was torn by him, by the variations in his words and actions. He shaded black to white and then back again, until she wanted to scream with vexation. Who was he? She never seemed to know. He was a mixture of odd parts, and so uneven, she could not comprehend him. And how could she ever marry a traitor to England?

Ambrose stood at the parlor window and pressed a hand against a considerably acidic stomach. It was nearly ten o'clock, and he was preparing to embark on a round of his favorite gaming establishments, but he could not be easy. He had received word only that morning from his contact in Portsmouth, confirming what Budgy had already told him—that the Frenchies were prepared to pay fifteen thousand pounds for the three articles Bracknell now had in his possession.

Fifteen thousand pounds! He could not even imagine where the French government, after so many years of revolution and war, had been able to amass such a sum.

His stomach bit at him, and he groaned slightly. He was dressed in burgundy satin knee breeches, the dark color accentuating his scrawny legs, while the thick padding of his dove-gray coat completed the picture of an awkward bird, a pigeon, as it were, to many of the gaming houses. A perfect pigeon who dropped his blunt with the ease of a greased wheel.

He was sorely agitated, uncertain what to do next. If he went to Portsmouth, he might possibly fall into the trap set for him, thereby losing his life, not to mention losing the Warfield fortune as well. But how could he pass up the opportunity of stealing fifteen thousand pounds? He could effect such a coup; he knew he could. But wouldn't it be wiser to remain where he was, to play his hand very close and safe?

Surely it would be very wise; But wisdom had never been his strong suit.

Wednesday had come so quickly, the days moving with the rapid speed of the Royal Mails. He had only to wait five more days, through Monday at midnight, and Warfield Hall would be his.

He had spoken to Ellen briefly that morning. She had been at Hookham's, dark circles beneath her eyes, her complexion pale. She had merely nodded in response to his questions. "Did Bracknell take the snuffbox?" She nodded once. "And were our suspicions confirmed?" A second nod and tears. Lord, she had become a watering pot, and he quit the premises as soon as he was able.

All he had to do was wait. But he was not used to waiting for anything. He despised the word. He wanted to act now, to do something to insure his success. He knew Lord Bracknell had left for Portsmouth early that morning, and by all appearances the viscount was now safely out of the way. All he had to do was make certain Ellen did not do anything foolish, did not even try to see Bracknell for five more days.

He laughed to himself at the thought of Ellen as a hackney coach pulled up in front of his town house. For all her abilities to manage the Hall, she was completely bird-witted where men were concerned. Moving into the hallway, he let Jaspar slip his cape over his shoulders. With cane in hand he slapped his very wide silk hat upon his head and gently tugged upon his neckcloth while Jaspar opened the door.

As he quit the town house, the cool, damp air flowed over him, and he laughed again. Poor cousin Ellen. Poor gullible Ellen. She had believed his lies and had looked for nothing further behind Lord Bracknell's activities. Faith, she deserved whatever fate handed to her in the next several days.

He felt safe because of Ellen's blindness yet not safe. Not completely, never completely. That was the rub. He wished to do something to make certain his plans would succeed.

As he climbed into the hackney, the leather seat and floor smelling sour and reeking of beer, he felt his stomach churn again at the opportunity he was giving up. Fifteen thousand pounds! And what if Ellen decided she would marry Bracknell anyway, spy or no? Then he would lose everything. No, he must begin hedging his bets as every smart gamester does. And he would begin with Ellen.

Rapping on the ceiling of the carriage, he called out, "Almack's, on King Street."

As they went down the country dance, Ellen shifted her gaze from Jeremy's face and took in her surroundings carefully. Usually she adored the pleasures of the assembly rooms, collecting her beaux about her with great zeal. But tonight all the joy was gone, and never had Almack's seemed so flat and insipid. The lemonade was sour beyond belief, and the little cake she attempted to consume in hopes of diverting her mind from a thousand unwelcome thoughts crumbled all over her ballgown of pale yellow silk. She even wished she had not worn her emeralds, for they only succeeded in reminding her of Bracknell and his emerald signet ring.

Jeremy seemed strangely nervous, his conversation coming in fits and starts. His gaze moved restlessly over the crowds, but often found a home upon Celeste's fair person. Even Celeste hardly appeared content. Several times when Ellen had caught her unawares, she found her sister frowning and chewing on her lower lip.

But at the moment Ellen did not care what was disturbing either of them, and she only half listened to the poet as they went down the dance. How relieved she was when the orchestra finished on a long note, and the tedious music was replaced by a general buzz of chattering laughter.

Jeremy bowed solemnly to her, and Ellen did not even remember whether she bowed in return. She wanted to go home. When they returned to Celeste and Laurie, she would have broached the subject immediately, but Laurence was holding up two very small round pieces of glass for Celeste's inspection, both of which looked a little like the glass used in spectacles, and was explaining that by merely holding them in a certain manner, one could create a telescopic effect. He was himself peering through the lenses at some distant object and gasped, "Good God! Why, who would have thought. Just saw old Marplot give Miss Goodwin a pinch right on her—"

He didn't complete the sentence, but the entire party turned to search for Miss Goodwin's willowy form and watched as the young lady scowled at Lord Marplot—an aged gentleman who was quite obviously in his cups—and turned haughtily away.

Celeste smiled faintly but appeared quite indifferent to both Laurie's lesson as well as to the fate of Mary Goodwin. Dark circles shadowed her pale blue eyes, and her skin seemed even more wan than usual except for an odd flush to her cheeks.

Sitting down beside her sister, Ellen, too, found little of interest in Mary's difficulties, and whispered, "Have you the headache, my dear? You look very tired."

Celeste sighed. "No. No, I am quite well."

Ellen merely patted her hand and sighed with her.

This time Celeste turned toward Ellen and smiled. "I might as well ask the same of you? Have you the headache?"

"It is not my head that hurts. It is my pride and my heart."

Celeste would have responded, but in that moment she caught sight of her husband's tall, thin form at the entrance to the assembly rooms and immediately leapt to her feet, insisting Jeremy dance with her. Laurie saw the cause of Celeste's sudden flight and moved a chair nearer to Ellen. Taking her arm in a protective fashion, he whispered to her, "Never fear, Miss Warfield. You may leave that fellow to me."

Ellen saw her cousin, his curly gold locks glistening with a slight oily sheen, and she wasn't sure what she felt. He had been the source of the most painful information she had ever received in her life—he had told her the truth about Bracknell. She should be grateful to him. But she still despised him for all the unhappiness he had caused Celeste.

She saw the expression of urgency on his face, and she wondered if he had news of Lord Bracknell. Suddenly she wished to speak with him more than anything else in the world.

Ambrose did not hesitate to make his way directly toward her and, ignoring Laurence, said, "I came only to have a word with you, Cousin." He then addressed Laurie, "And I shall not harm her; I promise!"

Ellen rose to her feet, now extremely anxious to hear what he had to say. Surely he had learned something. Perhaps the viscount had been apprehended by the militia and killed! She took Ambrose's proffered arm and bit back a thousand questions that tumbled across her mind. Instead she spoke in a quiet voice. "I have not seen Lord Bracknell since I gave him the snuffbox. Have you any word of him?"

"I can see you are very upset. I am sorry for you, Cousin." A sympathetic frown creased his brow as he looked down at her. "And I do have some news. I came to tell you I know for a fact he left for Portsmouth this morning. I suppose he means to sell your father's snuffbox and the two other articles to the French."

Ellen kept her gaze fixed on the hardwood floor in front of her. Tears had formed in her eyes, and she did not want anyone to see her distress. So, Bracknell had already left. "You were right," she uttered in hushed tones. "Lord Bracknell spoke of his debts and of solving his financial difficulties by . . . " She could not say it.

"You are very much in love with him, are you not?"

Ellen did not answer.

"Ah, I understand. I do. But I wanted you to know what has happened, that he has indeed gone. You must be in a state of the severest agitation. Again, I feel most acutely for you."

Ellen did not know what to say as they made a slow progress about the ballroom floor. When she had blinked back her tears, she nodded to various of her acquaintances, most of whom seemed surprised she was actually strolling about the ballroom with a cousin she was known to despise.

But she was oblivious of any of their stares. She only wanted Ambrose to tell her more, to tell her everything.

"Couldn't there have been some mistake?" she asked.

He squeezed her arm gently. "I'm afraid not. Why, all of London knows he is a gamester of the worst sort and that Three Elms is soon to be sold."

"Sold?" Ellen was shocked. Did Bracknell think she would permit him to repair his fortunes through the Warfield estate? How little he knew her, then. She would starve first.

Ambrose said, "I should never sell Warfield Hall, were I master there. I know my duty to my country and to my progeny."

These words flowed over Ellen, burning her soul. Duty to one's country and progeny. She looked up at her cousin, his face contorted in an emotion she knew suited him well. Bitterness. And he was lying. Even to himself he was lying. He would lose the Hall within a year. He was no better than Bracknell save in one thing—at least Ambrose, for all the massive flaws of his character, was not a traitor.

She shivered slightly, and he asked in a gentle voice if she had taken a chill. When she replied she was quite comfortable, he began relating in a subdued voice all he knew of Bracknell—how many times he had seen the man gaming at Stratfield's, of the largess he had wasted at Newmarket. He dwelled upon every incident where Bracknell had flaunted the telegraph fan, telling anyone who would listen about how he hoped to secure the fortune of the golden heiress.

Ellen's spirits sank lower and lower. Releasing Ambrose's arm, she said, "How grateful I am that my eyes have been opened to that man's character. You have saved me from a terrible fate. I only wish I could help my country."

Ambrose pressed her arm and said, "Do not concern yourself with that. I intend to go to Portsmouth myself and see if I can be of any assistance to the authorities."

She said, "And I always thought you had no feeling, cousin. But here I discover a gentleman of true patriotic fervor."

Ambrose left Almack's shortly afterward, extremely pleased with his efforts. Ellen was certainly as foolish as ever, so there was nothing more to do but while away the early-morning hours gambling. At Mrs. Stratfield's he lost two hundred pounds, punting on tick, and another hundred at a seamy little place to the east of Mayfair. Life was sweet, and he was so well satisfied with his conversation with Ellen, he got himself thoroughly foxed.

Chapter Twelve

ON THURSDAY MORNING, with only a little more than four days remaining in which to fulfill the conditions of the will, Ellen sat quietly before the fireplace in her bedroom, her golden ringlets trailing in an ill-combed mass down her back. In her right hand she held the special license and in her left a note from Celeste. Never, in her entire life, had she known such enormous sadness.

The April morning was cold, the dampness creeping beneath the windowsill and spreading a clammy coldness upon every unguarded surface. Ellen took care against the cold, sitting with a warm shawl thrown over her nightdress and a woolen blanket across her knees. But the fire and the shawl and the blanket could not relieve the chill that had encased her heart.

Dear Celeste! Her sister's letter was not hastily composed, as had been the one written to her seven years ago when Celeste was but fifteen, but written carefully and marred only by faded gray splotches, a christening of tears.

Celeste had eloped with Jeremy. They had left at five o'clock in the morning, sneaking away like schoolchildren to a Maying, and were heading first to Dower House to retrieve the boys. They would live in Scotland forever. Celeste was sorry, terribly sorry, and despised being parted from Ellen so brutally, but she loved Jeremy. He was everything Ambrose was not, and she meant to have a life filled with as much love as she could manage, and Jeremy loved her.

Had they any hope for happiness? Ellen wasn't certain. But she was comforted by one part of the letter where Celeste spoke with a maturity that surprised Ellen. *He loves me, even with my faults, which you yourself know so well —I am pitiably dependent on the kindness of others for my happiness, and I haven't the least will when it comes to the raising and guidance of my sons. But I mean to do better, and Jeremy promises me he will try not to let his poetic furors spill into our family life together.*

There was enough for hope in those lines, she thought. But an elopement! Another scandal, while her own world was being reshaped by a wind so strong, she didn't know how to withstand its force.

Ellen stared into the fire. The coals, pink and white, mesmerized her. Was this a nightmare from which she would soon awaken? Oh, if only that were true. Thoughts of Celeste led to visions of her dandified cousin, to Bracknell smiling mischievously at her, to memories of how his declaration of love had engulfed her so completely. She leaned back in the chair, the special license and Celeste's letter falling to the carpet at her feet. It was all of nine o'clock in the morning, but she felt as fatigued as if it were midnight. She wished she might lose herself in sleep, but sleep was an elusive creature, which, even last night, had led her a hard, pounding chase. She had awakened with the bedclothes twisted all about her and her head still full of terrible nightmares, dreams of having been bound up by a thief and left to die in one of the attics at Warfield Hall.

Again the question beat itself upon her disquieted mind: Why had her papa inflicted this upon her? Would he have wittingly wished so much pain upon her? How could such a wise man have been so wrong about one of his friends?

The door opened, creaking slightly upon its hinges, and Ellen opened her eyes to see Becky standing in the doorway, an expression of concern wrinkling the maid's freckled forehead. In her arms she carried a tray, and entering the warm chamber, she said quietly, "La, but it's lovely in here. Even the hallway is like to freeze my bum off."

Ellen normally would have rebuked her sharply, but today she did not have room in her heart to care about her maid's coarseness.

The worried crease on Becky's brow deepened. "Not even a smile?"

"I daresay this morning life will go on without me if I do not smile. I do not feel like smiling. Nor do I have the least appetite. You may eat the food yourself."

The frown on Becky's face disappeared, and she sat down on the floor immediately, leaning against the bed-frame and setting the tray over her lap. "I thank you very much. You know that cook of yours don't fix enough food for the servants. Why, I'm like to starve."

Ellen could not restrain a smile as her own servant, completely oblivious of matters such as decorum and proper behavior, poured a dish of jam over a thin slice of bread. She was a very healthy-looking creature with wide hips, and Ellen could not keep from responding, "Yes, I can see you are slowly fading from sight."

Becky laughed. "That's better! There's a sparkle in your eye now!"

"You are incorrigible, you know."

"I never pretended otherwise."

Ellen looked at her squarely and announced, "Celeste eloped with Jeremy Andover this morning."

"And I wish them happy, for she married an ugly customer, and she deserves far better than the likes of that mealymouthed muckworm!" Jam trailed down her fingers, and she licked them with complete abandon.

Ellen grimaced. "Have you no manners at all?"

Becky grinned. "None. T'other servants can't abide me in the kitchens. La, what an uppity lot you've hired here."

"I don't know why I tolerate your impudence."

"I don't know either," she responded cheerfully.

"Are you never out of frame."

"Oh, sometimes, if I've been in one place too long. You know, I've always wanted to travel, like to New South Wales. I knew a couple of coves what sailed there. Of course I never heard from them again, but I often wondered what they were doing. They wanted to raise sheep. Of course," and here Ellen noticed Becky's eyes shift slightly, "you've got to be strong for that sort of life. You can't let others tell you what to do and when to do it and take everybody's word for the truth, if you see what I mean. You've got to push your way a little, like Celeste has. Not that I'm saying she's done right, but she seems to know what's right for her. That's an unusual quality. And if a person were to go to a new country, he's got to see things that way. You've really got to know what's right for you, and then just do it, no matter how much anyone complains about it or says it ain't right, or proper, or anything really prosy like that. Why, you get left behind when you think like that. You live your life trying to please a bunch of people who don't give a fig for you anyway. No, were Celeste to emigrate to America or somewhere else, she'd do fine. She would. And so would I. At least I think I would."

Ellen shifted her feet, a little uncomfortable with what her maid was saying, and felt one of her slippers catch the special license and slide it along the carpet. She said, "I think Miss Becky Lovedean would do splendidly whatever she did or wherever she went. I only wonder that you've chosen a serving occupation. You seem to have great abilities. I wonder that you never performed upon the stage."

Becky choked on her tea, and finally sputtered, "I . . . I could never abide the thought of standing up in front of so many people like that!"

Ellen was a little surprised at her maid's reaction, and she wondered for a moment if Becky had at one time performed upon the stage. She thought it highly probably. But what did it matter? What did anything matter, for in a few days, she would be impoverished, and Ambrose would begin tearing Warfield Hall apart, debt by debt.

Ellen regarded Becky with a curious expression. Did she truly long to start a new life in a country as wild as New South Wales? Ellen tried to imagine what such a life would be like, and she could only shudder. She had always wanted to travel, but not in poverty, and not with the truly difficult task before her of beginning life anew, with little but her youth and her health. She was not made of such stern stuff as Becky was—her maid would flourish no matter where she rested her head. But what was Becky really trying to tell her?

When Becky was done licking her fingers clean, and had drunk the entire pot of tea, Ellen began her toilette, musing several times over what her maid had said. And during the course of the morning, as she walked aimlessly about the rooms, inspecting the staff's cleaning efforts, her thoughts turned often to Celeste and to Bracknell. A sudden shower hit the windows and softened to a steady rain, darkening the town house for the entire afternoon. The dreary weather became a fine excuse for her—she was hardly in a mood to receive visitors, nor did she wish to leave the comfort of her drawing room.

The day wore on as she sat curled up on the settee in front of the fire, her thoughts in continual motion across the full canvas of her difficulties. She tried as best she could to ignore most of her sadness and hurt as well as the growing fears for her future, and instead focused on all that Becky had said to her—lessons of survival.

The gray skies turned black, the rain a dull pounding on the roof as the hour turned from evening to night. She did not know precisely when the idea struck her, but she thought it might have been between bites of lobster patty and creamed peas as she sat alone in the morning room toying with her dinner. The idea was so simple in its structure and so perfect, she wondered where it had come from, for truly it was an inspiration of no small magnitude.

Her heart began beating loudly in her ears, as a sense of excitement drew her from her lethargy, and with increased speed she consumed the remaining lobster patty, poached turbot, peas, and a saucer full of raspberries and cream.

One thing was certain: Had Celeste not eloped with Jeremy, she would never have had considered effecting a scheme that had self-interest as its central feature.

That was Becky's message—society strictures were adequate for the ordinary events of one's life, but when the extraordinary or unbearable occurred, then courage was what was needed. Particularly when it meant flying in the face of public criticism and horror, for her schemes would no doubt effect one of the worst scandals of the decade.

And she did possess courage. After all, she was Papa's daughter.

Her heart positively sang with relief that she was finally doing something about this dreadful fix she was in, instead of sitting and waiting for fate to descend upon her like an ugly vulture intent upon devouring her while she was but half-alive.

She knew precisely what to do, and though it was eight in the evening, she began gathering her forces together. And at seven the next morning, she was fully dressed in traveling clothes, pulling on her lavender kid gloves and supervising the arrangement of all the bandboxes she and Becky had packed the night before.

She checked yet again to make certain she had the special license with her and read his lordship's name and hers —if not with pleasure, then at least with relief—tied her purple bonnet carefully over her blond curls, pinched her cheeks, and quit the town house.

The smooth London streets gave way to the rough rock of England's extensive turnpike system, and they were soon on the road to Portsmouth.

Ellen sat with her head high, feeling more confident than she had in a long time. Even Becky smiled at her, nodded approvingly and something a little more—Becky seemed considerably relieved, the rather forced smiles of the last few days having given way to that gap-toothed grin that always won an answering smile in return.

Glancing out the window, Ellen hoped by the time they arrived in Portsmouth, they would be able to find Lord Bracknell quickly. For even though it was only Friday and she had until Monday to marry him, still, she did not wish to tempt fate again.

The coach rattled and swayed toward Portsmouth, and every change of horses brought a brief respite, the ladies descending the post chaise to walk about the yard. But so quickly was the transfer made that it seemed once they had stepped down from the coach it was nearly time to remount.

Ellen did not mind the rigors of traveling at all. No carriage sickness assailed her, and though they were heartily bounced about when a hole in the road surprised them every now and again, all in all the journey was tolerably pleasant. That is, as long as Ellen did not dwell on what she was about to do. Oh, but she did not wish to think of the frightening duty she would have to perform, for she had already decided to take Lord Bracknell to the navy office once she had married him. The thought that he would hang for his treachery caused every part of her body to ache, and with a sinking sensation she realized yet again just how much she loved him.

Ellen closed her eyes as the post chaise bowled across the chalk downs of Hampshire, and the smell of sea air began drifting into the carriage. She would not think about Bracknell's fate, concentrating instead on the fact that in less than a day, her task would be complete, and she could retire to Warfield Hall, her future secure.

When Ellen finally opened her eyes as the fragrant, salty breezes freshened the coach, she cried "Good heavens!" for the view opened up to a thicket of masts and a tumble of red roofs. "Portsmouth," she whispered, and her heart lurched within her as though it, too, were attached to the same indifferent springs of the swaying coach. "So many ships!"

"It always looks like that," Becky said, her voice oddly reverent. "A white-masted graveyard. Each time I see the harbor, the masts look like so many crosses floating on the sea. Not close up as we'll soon be, but now, seeing them above the rooftops."

The sun had began to set, and the ocean and the ships were soon swathed in a red glow. Long, black shadows merged between the ships, and a fog bank had begun curling into the harbor. Ellen suddenly felt terrified as the thick mist swallowed up the rose-colored ships. That was how she felt—consumed by events that had nothing to do with her.

In a few minutes they were rattling down the long High Street, and once they passed through the white stone arch of the ancient fortifications, a scant two minutes saw them pull before The George Inn where Lord Nelson was known to have drunk his tea. Portsmouth overwhelmed her in that moment as she descended from the coach. Hundreds of dock men from the docks were crowding the narrow streets, finishing their day's labor and returning home. The port smelled of salt air and fish, and the encroaching mist added to the thick dampness of the air. The noise of the port and the courtyard of the coaching inn, were jumbled together, the shouts of the postboys ringing in her ears as she headed for the inn.

An old sailor with a black patch over one eye and thick gray brows sat smoking a pipe at the entrance to The George. He leered at Ellen as she passed by, which served to increase the fear that had her locked securely in its grip. She refused to look at him, but heard his hoarse laughter as she took a step sideways to keep the skirts of her lavender pelisse from brushing his arm.

Becky followed behind her, and only after Ellen had advanced several feet into the inn did she realize that her maid had actually stopped to speak to the old man.

Ellen called to her sharply and thought yet again that Becky ought to curb her appetites a little more and that flirting with a dirty old man like the one posted at the door was certainly scraping the very bottom of the barrel.

When Becky caught up with her, Ellen whispered, "You might have at least waited until we were settled in our chambers before you began collecting your beaux!"

"Whatever for?" she said in an excited whisper. "What a feisty cove that one is! He wanted to know what time I'd be putting you to bed, and would I like to see the bathing machines at Portsea by night? I would have been greatly offended by his impertinence had his suggestion not sounded like just the sort of lark I am always game for!"

Ellen responded in a hushed voice, "Despicable creature! Why do I keep you about me?"

Becky laughed. "That's better. You don't look so scared now. And don't be such a simpleton, Miss Ellen. Think, for a moment—who would know the whereabouts of our man better than that old salty sitting out there day and night. Likes he knows everyone here in Portsmouth."

Ellen glanced over her shoulder and realized the truth of Becky's words. Looking back at her maid, she had the very odd thought that Becky had a scheme of her own going flicker lightly across her mind. But indeed that was too absurd for words. What could her maid possibly be up to? Was she now seeing traitorous shadows in every familiar face? And she laughed at her own stupidity. "You are a very clever female, Miss Becky Lovedean. I now only wonder if perhaps I should meet your sailor at the bathing machines tonight in your stead."

She laughed aloud at the shock on Becky's face. Truly she was a little surprised she had said something so completely brazen, but her maid deserved it. One thing, however, was certain, a friendship with such a man would do them no harm.

On the following morning Ellen sat before a very small mahogany table and opened the lid of a beautiful wood case containing her father's favorite dueling pistols. The case smelled faintly of her papa, a familiar fragrance of soap and leather. The scent reached out to her, startling her and a wave of grief poured over her, one memory after another leaping to the front of her mind. Her throat constricted harshly as she leaned her forehead upon the edge of the open case. If only Papa were here. He could settle everything in a trice! But her father wasn't here, and she must do what she thought best.

For several moments she sat thus, her head pressed against the case. Her eyes were clouded with so much feeling, she could barely see the table upon which her gaze was fixed. But this would not do! She had too many tasks of import to accomplish. Becky had been gone for nearly an hour in search of their quarry, and this thought brought her firmly back to her present task. It was Saturday—only two days remained in which to secure her inheritance.

Ellen removed both long-muzzled pistols from the nest of red velvet in the elegant wood case and began rubbing them with a clean linen handkerchief, just as she had seen her papa do a thousand times. She had always hated firearms, and though he had wanted to teach her to shoot, she had refused. She hated the noise. It seemed a strange incongruity in her that she could ride to hounds like the devil was at her back, but she couldn't bear the sight or sound of pistols or sporting guns.

She had watched her papa load the pistols several times and she carefully set about repeating the process. She hoped she remembered to do everything properly. After pouring the powder into the barrel, she tamped the pistol ball securely next to the powder. All else, to her somewhat inexperienced eyes, seemed to be in order, but she wasn't really sure. And she was surprised at the weight of the firearm. Could she possibly guard her prisoner for hours at a time? Leveling the pistol at the curtains, her sights set on a small cobweb in the corner of the window, she wondered what shattering glass would sound like, and whether or not she would have to fire the pistol in order to force Bracknell to marry her.

The door opened and Becky walked in quickly, saying, "I hope you know how to use that thing. I've found Lord Bracknell, and you'd best not waste a minute. He's enjoying a hearty breakfast at the Fountain. If you catch him now, you'll not have the least difficulty in sweeping him into the post chaise."

Lord Bracknell sat deep in thought, his knife and fork poised over a thick slice of ham. He had not received word that Ambrose had arrived, and he wondered if too much in that respect had been left up to chance. Why should Hazeley follow him to Portsmouth and risk exposure by struggling with another man for possession of the coded articles? No person of sense would do so, however large the rewards.

This was the first time he had been left so completely uniformed as to the total plan for the operation. He was only grateful Ellen was safely in London. For some time he had been afraid she would become entangled, however unwittingly, in this fast-approaching conclusion to her cousin's treachery.

With that reassuring thought, he attacked the slice of smoked ham and drank his coffee. Damn and blast, but time was running out. Ellen needed him back by Monday at the latest, and here it was Saturday. As he drained his cup, a servant brought the note he had been waiting for. Ambrose had been seen at The George. His task of the moment was to let Hazeley see he was in Portsmouth, then return to the Fountain to await further instructions.

Bracknell felt tense with excitement. All the pieces were falling neatly into place, though he was still a little amazed the gamester had followed him to Portsmouth at all.

Rising quickly from his seat, Lord Bracknell left the dining room in time to catch the servant by the arm and ask who had delivered the letter. The servant responded an old man with a black patch over his eye had brought it not five minutes ago. Well-satisfied, the viscount crossed the threshold, took a deep breath of sea air, and prepared to complete his mission. However, he had not taken three steps onto the flags when a female walked up to him, stood very close, and shoved something hard against his ribs.

"Ellen!" he cried, and would have pushed the object away from his chest had he not looked down and with amazement seen she held a dueling pistol in her hand.

He thought he heard an odd, muffled laughter coming from within the inn, but it was abruptly replaced by a series of harsh barking coughs. A familiar sound, he thought. But where had he heard it before?

He was about to ask his love what she meant by this attack upon his person when Ellen whispered, "Remain silent, Lord Bracknell, and I shall spare your life." He could feel she was trembling, and he felt a very real perspiration bead up on his own brow at the thought of her nerves communicating an unwanted command to the trigger. But as he looked down at the pistol, he saw there was no flint in the flintlock mechanism, and he nearly burst out laughing.

Swallowing his amusement, which was very difficult given the fierce expression on his love's face, he found his eyes watering from the effort. He nodded slowly, and only when he knew he could keep his countenance did he venture to speak. "I'm not certain I understand why you are here, dearest. Was it something I said?"

"I am not speaking to you, my lord traitor, and you may dispense with the endearments. I will not be bamboozled again."

"Ah."

"Ah," she repeated sarcastically, keeping her voice low. "You are now my prisoner, and I mean to turn you over to the navy office, but not until you have performed a certain duty."

"And that is?"

"To marry me, of course. I never told you this, and perhaps you have already guessed as much, but my father specified one gentleman only who could fulfill the terms of his will."

"Me?" he asked, considerably surprised. What on earth had Vincent been thinking? He knew Warfield would go to any length to achieve his desires, but why had he wanted Ellen to marry him? Unless it was for the title, but then that was not old Warfield at all. There was only one answer, knowing Vincent as he did—the old man had thought they should suit, and he was right. Damme, he was right! But how he was to proceed out of this coil with Hazeley's affair drawing to a close he couldn't imagine.

A post chaise arrived at that moment with a freckled female present who looked unmistakably familiar to Bracknell. Red curls peeped from beneath a black hood, and he knew he had seen her before, not just in Ellen's presence as her maid, but in another setting entirely. But where? And when? Then he recognized her.

Cleopatra! His eyes opened wide in surprise. Vincent had planned everything exceedingly well. The maid had been placed not only to protect Ellen, but also to deliver his messages. But what should he do now? Even if Ellen had been properly armed, he could have taken the pistol away from her with scarcely a blink of an eye, and he was tempted to do just that.

But he didn't want to. She appeared so beautiful and confused, standing on the busy flagways of Portsmouth holding her father's dueling pistol, that it was all he could do to keep from ravishing her then and there. And the delight of seeing his errant fiancée was so great, he was prepared to leave the bustling harbor on the instant just to be with her—hang Hazeley and the Frenchies. Not for the world did he want to escape whatever scheme Ellen had now concocted, foolish chit!

Regarding the maid with a thoughtful glance, he saw in response the smallest nod, and so, rather than take the pistol from Ellen, he did not hesitate to clamber into the coach beside the red-haired servant.

Ellen stood on the flagway not knowing precisely what she should do. She held the pistol, now grown exceedingly heavy in hand, and kept it partially concealed beneath her cape. But how was she to keep it leveled at her prisoner and at the same time mount the coach?

And worse, the rake seemed perfectly aware of her difficulty and sat smiling broadly at her, his expression one of smug satisfaction as he sat beside Becky, his arms folded across his chest. The scoundrel! If only that stupid gleam in his eye would settle down a trifle, she might feel more confidence in this wretched abduction.

When she remained on the flagway, her brow knit in consternation, he suggested, "Perhaps your maid could hold the pistol while you climb into the coach? And I should be happy to assist you." He extended a hand hopefully.

Ellen wanted to say something quite witty, but no such eloquence came to mind. And after hesitating for only a moment, she gave the pistol to Becky, and, pushing her cape over her shoulder, took Bracknell's hand and ascended the vehicle. A light rain began dotting the flagways, then a stiff ocean breeze brought a burst of rain smattering the top of the carriage. She was grateful to be safely inside, though a little disconcerted at having Bracknell so close to her.

Retrieving the pistol from Becky, Ellen gave the postilion the direction to proceed, and the town chariot pulled quickly into the flow of traffic. Within a scant few minutes, the small wedding party was rumbling along the High Street and heading toward the small village of Southwick, some three miles north of Portsmouth.

Bracknell hummed the entire way, even when Ellen asked him politely to be quiet, informing him the scratchy noises he emitted were having a contrary effect upon her nerves. He responded that he always hummed when he was frightened out of his wits, which only made Ellen mad as fire, for he looked about as frightened as a little boy who has just discovered a new penny.

They were crowded together, the three of them, and Ellen only wished Becky had been placed between them. As it was, he complained loudly about his captors not providing a more commodious vehicle and about not having enough room, shifting sideways slightly so he was turned toward Ellen, his knees forcibly crushing her own. Throwing an arm over the back of her seat, he then began playing with several wayward curls at the nape of her neck, which had freed themselves from the confines of her bonnet.

"Stop this at once," she cried, and tried to slap his hand away, but he persisted.

"Your golden ringlets have tormented me since that night at Vauxhall. Do you remember that evening?"

"Yes; you behaved scandalously!"

"As I recall, you did not complain too loudly at the time." He twisted a curl about his finger. "And you were gowned in such a fashion as to bring out the very worst in me." He touched the nape of her neck, and a shiver traveled all the way down her spine, somehow finding its way to the tips of her toes.

"Would you please stop that," she said, a little less forcefully than before.

"Impossible. As long as we are traveling in this ridiculous fashion, I shall do as I please."

"You are a rogue."

"And we are to be married, so you should be pleased rather than offended that I admire your hair." He turned his head slightly and addressed Becky over his shoulder: "You must forgive me for ignoring you, but if I don't gentle her, she will be impossible on our wedding night."

This was too much for Ellen, who was feeling an extreme frustration at the feelings he evoked in her, and without thinking she lifted her gloved hand and slapped him on the cheek.

"Miss Ellen," Becky cried in a startled voice, as Portsmouth gave way to the surrounding countryside.

Ellen burst into tears, the pistol now lying useless on her lap. "Oh, Hugh, I'm sorry, but why have you done this terrible thing?"

He took her gently in his arms and cradled her. "I know you didn't mean it. Only, why are you so upset? I thought all was settled between us. Why did you come to Portsmouth when I told you I would be back in time to marry you?"

Ellen now felt torn between pulling away from him and staying within the circle of his arms. She chose for the moment to stay, and sniffling, said, "Because I felt it was my duty to take you to the navy office and let them deal with you as they must. You see, I know what you mean to do with my kerchief, fan, and Papa's snuffbox."

An oddly strangled sound issued from his throat. She knew he must be very upset now that he realized she was aware of his traitorous schemes.

He finally said, "I see. Well, then I suppose nothing more can be said now that you know all. But I mean to go peacefully, seeing you are intent upon doing your duty, and will be happy to oblige you by marrying you first. There is only one thing I wish to know . . ."

Since he hesitated, Ellen lifted her gaze to him, her eyes

full of tears, and was grateful that he dried her cheeks. His expression, however, was one of amusement, and she asked quietly, "Yes, what is it, Hugh?"

In a cheerful tone, he asked, "Do you mean to attend my execution?"

Ellen was horrified. How could he speak so flippantly to her about so miserable a subject? And the very thought of him—oh, dear, she would not permit the gruesome picture to form in her mind, of gallows and gawking crowds! She was so upset at his lack of sensibility, for a moment she could hardly speak.

Pulling away from him, she again drew the pistol from her lap and leveled it at his chest. Apparently he did not take her seriously, for she could see by the glimmer of amusement in his eye, he thought it all a great joke.

And poor Becky. Her maid was doubled over, sobbing into her skirts at the tragedy of the situation, and here was Lord Bracknell, funning!

"What a wretched man you are! Don't think for a moment, my lord, I will not give you to the authorities."

He shrugged. "I am lost, then."

Ellen narrowed her eyes at him and tried to look fierce. "And you deserve for me to finish you off right here and now. Only, look how poor Becky is suffering."

Bracknell regarded the maid, her hooded curls still buried within the skirts of her gown, and he turned to pat her shoulder. "There, there, Becky. I am sorry if I have caused you any grief. Do you mean to attend the hanging as well?"

This sent Becky bending further into her skirts, and Ellen reproached Bracknell with one final glaring scowl. Then, averting her gaze, she turned to watch the rain shape and reshape itself on the front windowglass of the post chaise.

Silence fell within the confines of the coach, and after half an hour the carriage drew into the village and headed directly to the vicarage. They descended quickly and were greeted by an astonished maid, who, seeing the pistol in Ellen's hand, gave a loud shriek. This brought an elderly vicar, his spectacles in hand, rushing to the entrance hall, along with the cook and a small scullery maid.

Forcing Bracknell into the hall, and seeing that Becky shut the door against the cold, spring rain, Ellen spoke first. "I am sorry to disturb you in this hurly-burly fashion, but I am Miss Warfield of Warfield Hall, and this is Lord Bracknell, and we . . . we must marry immediately. It is most urgent." She handed the pistol to Becky, who kept it pointed at the handsome peer, and Ellen withdrew the special license from her reticule. She took a deep breath, trying to settle her pounding heart, and handed the official document to the vicar.

He scratched his balding head, still considerably astonished, and read the license carefully. Regarding Lord Bracknell intently, he asked, "Have you been abducted, sir, against your will?"

"No, not entirely. I had hoped for a more solemn ceremony, but this lady and I are indeed affianced." He gestured to Ellen. "As you can see, her love for me is so great, she could not wait until tomorrow when we would have been married at a more comfortable time."

The clergyman turned disbelieving eyes upon Ellen. "Were you to be married tomorrow, indeed?"

"I had hoped to be, but I discovered I could not rely entirely upon this man's character, and was afraid he would not fulfill his obligation to me. He . . . he has got me with child! My case is most desperate!"

Everyone, including the maid, who had never left the entrance hall, turned to stare at Ellen. Even Becky gasped.

"He is a rake, my good sir," she continued. "He seduced me completely, and now I insist you marry us at once. I . . . I wish to have my baby within the very respectable bonds of wedlock."

Lord Bracknell promptly fell into whoops, as did Becky, and the poor vicar began taking on the severe expression of one who believes he is the brunt of some tasteless joke. He began to expostulate on the very wicked morals of this modern generation, but Bracknell interrupted him, "No . . . no, my good sir. Pray, marry us at once, for if you don't, I shall elope with her to Gretna Green, and certainly that will not do."

The vicar, now scowling at them both, was ready to turn them away, but Ellen, seeing his hesitation, cried, "Pray, sir, I am desperate. You don't know what this man is, and I must marry him today!"

He stared long and hard at her and seemed to weigh the situation carefully. "I believe your feelings have overpowered you, miss, er, Miss Warfield, but wouldn't your parents wish you to be married from their home? Have you discussed your . . . your situation with them?"

Ellen wished more than anything he had not spoken these words, for they nearly undid her. In a quiet voice she replied, "My parents are both dead. And . . . and if I am not married today, there are conditions attached to my inheritance that would impoverish me forever."

The mention of her inheritance seemed to have a very strange effect upon the vicar, for his cheeks grew quite red and even the cook, a large wooden spoon in her hand, drew in her breath. The vicar nodded curtly and said "Come with me."

As they walked into the parlor, he said, "If parents only knew how wicked such conditions upon an inheritance can be . . . " He stood before the window rocking on his heels, the gray light behind him casting his face in shadow. "I had been the rightful heir to a property in Kent, but a single clause, overlooked by a very incompetent solicitor that I be married by the time I was five and twenty—" He broke off nearly apoplectic with rage. And only after he had brought his temper under control and his breathing settled into a more normal rhythm, was he able to continue, "—and there was nothing that could be done. No justice in England over such an absurdity." He regarded Ellen from ferocious blue eyes. "If such is your case, were this man a libertine and a traitor to our country, I would join you in matrimony. Nothing should separate a man, or woman, from his lawful inheritance."

When the ceremony was complete, Ellen told the vicar there was no need to sanctify the union with a kiss since she and her husband would never be seeing each other again. The clergyman seemed satisfied with this and bowed solemnly to her, wishing her well, and stood ready to usher the party toward the door.

Ellen had just taken the pistol from Becky when Bracknell said, "One moment, Miss Warfield. This will not do." And he stopped everyone in progress. "If I do not have the kiss that is due me for taking part in this ceremony, I shan't return peaceably to Portsmouth. You will have to kill me first."

Ellen gasped. "Don't be absurd."

"And don't be such a gudgeon, my love." Regardless of the weapon she was pointing at his chest, he pulled her into his arms and kissed her quite thoroughly, much to the shock of the assembled witnesses.

Ellen again felt that sweet sensation of being in his arms, which ruled her heart more completely than even the laws of heaven. How was it possible he could make her forget everything except that she loved him by merely melding his body with hers and cradling her head with a very gentle hand? How she loved him—the scent of his skin, the awful strength of his arms, the way he would ignore every propriety and kiss her in front of a group of strangers.

Ellen let the pistol dangle at her side and, very faintly, even though she was absorbed completely in the gentle pressure of his lips and the pull of his arm about her waist as he held her very close to him, did she hear a little thump when it hit the carpet.

"Good gracious, whatever will happen next?" a rich country voice, the cook's, rang out.

The couple parted, and Ellen followed everyone's gaze and saw beside her the pistol ball and a patch of black powder staining the carpet. "Oh, no!" she cried.

Becky could not contain her laughter and moved well into the entrance hall where she gave way to her mirth. The cook began scolding both the maids and insisting they clean the powder up immediately, and Lord Bracknell picked up the useless weapon.

Handing it back to her, he said with a smile, "And now, my love, shall we return to Portsmouth?"

Ellen tilted her head, her eyes wide with astonishment. "But . . . but, now that I have no weapon, surely you will try to escape?"

"Whatever for? Of the moment I wish only to do your bidding, and to end this horrid business that has kept us apart for these three interminable days."

"But, Hugh—" she cried. "You will end up on Tyburn Tree." And she threw her arms about his neck.

What could he do but kiss her again and hold her very hard? When she finally released him, he said, "You were very right, however, that we must now return to Portsmouth." He could not resist adding, "We must think of the baby, mustn't we?"

Ellen pulled slightly away from him a little bemused and then blushed scarlet. "Yes, oh, yes, of course."

Never in her entire life had Ellen felt so low as when she emerged from the navy office. Lord Bracknell had been taken away immediately, and she was rewarded for her efforts by being forced to take a vow of silence, along with Becky and all the officers present. The officers told her matters had reached an alarming state in Portsmouth with an influx of French agents over the past two years, and her dearest husband was believed to be one of the most notorious agents among them. They all looked very nervous as they stood about, shifting their feet. But they thanked Ellen again and again, telling her she had done very well and they were on the brink of breaking up the most devious network that had ever infected the harbor region since the Battle of Trafalgar. She was then instructed to return to London, and for the sake of her country's future, never to speak of her adventures again. As if she could!

Becky tried to lift her spirits. "There, there, miss. You've done the right thing. After all, he was selling secrets to the French, and now that you've married him, you can live at Warfield Hall, all alone, and one day die of old age."

"What a delightful thought, Becky," Ellen responded quietly. "How you do ease the burn in my heart. I only wonder I didn't think of it before."

Chapter Thirteen

"AND YOU WITNESSED the ceremony yourself?" Ambrose stood very still, the only sound in his chamber the measured ticking of his watch.

Becky stood near the door, watching the indifferent, almost emotionless cast to his features. She was guarding her exit, aware that the creature before her was capable of anything. He had no conscience whatsoever. "Aye, there was nothing I could do. She had a pistol with her, though she didn't even notice the flint was missing." She laughed harshly. "But they are married."

Ambrose regarded her in a searching fashion, his green-gold eyes flashing darts of anger, as he said with a lilt to his voice, "Then she must perish—mysteriously, of course—for I have grown extremely fond of the notion of possessing Warfield Hall."

Becky suppressed a shudder and, using every trained dramatic ability she possessed, kept her features schooled to a mild indifference. She said, "I don't care what happens to her, Mr. Hazeley. She's turned me off without a reference, and I've nowhere to go now. I've done right by you, and all I want is the emerald ring. I'm for New South Wales in a few weeks."

"And you may rest assured I shall keep my promise once I am master of the Hall." He smiled generously upon her. "I think we have a great deal in common, you and I. All we each want is an opportunity, don't you agree?"

Never, Becky thought, had she agreed less with anyone. In the course of her service to Vincent, she had met a great many people involved in every sort of chicanery. But Ambrose Hazeley was in a class all by himself—sinister and completely without the least regard for anyone but himself, quite willing to speak of murdering his own cousin, and that without a single blink of his large eyes.

"That's right," she echoed him. "We both have been cheated by fate. But I mean to change all that. I heard from one of the servants at the Fountain that Bracknell means to quit the inn tonight, so he must be planning to sell the information today."

"And where, then, is Lord Bracknell?" he asked.

"As you may well imagine, the navy office spewed him out not an hour after his capture. He's at his inn now. I followed him there after Miss Ellen dismissed me. But I don't know what to do next."

"First, you will go to the Fountain and wait. Watch Bracknell's movements, and when he leaves the inn, you are to report immediately back to me. I don't think it shall be very long, however, for a friend of mine has just sent word they've set a trap for Lord Bracknell and they expect him in Broad Street within the hour. Go at once, and when he leaves, bring a hackney back to The George. We shall take Ellen to the good viscount and deal with them together. A romantic honeymoon, I think. Another yachting accident at sea. How very fitting. And how fortuitous that I should be staying at the same inn as my cousin. I shall, however, be waiting across the street for your arrival. I don't want Ellen to see you again; we shan't risk a chance encounter here."

When he had finished delivering his instructions, Becky dipped a small curtsy and quit the room. Only when she was in the hallway did she pause, squeezing her eyes shut, to dispel the fear that had gripped her spirit for the entire length of the interview. Did he suspect treachery in her? She hadn't the least idea.

Picking up her skirts, she hurried to find a hackney and headed to the Fountain. There she found the old sailor, who listened with delight to everything she told him, grinning with an expression close to madness.

Bracknell had been watching the street for an hour, when he finally saw the person he thought would return—the old, weather-beaten sailor who bore a patch over one eye. He had been told to wait for a message, and from the upstairs room, he had a clear view. He watched the sailor enter the inn and return to the street a few minutes later, so he was not surprised when there was a knock on the door shortly thereafter.

The note he received was simple. *Proceed to Broad Street and gain admittance to the house bearing a model ship in the left front parlor window. Ask for Charles. Go in a friendly manner bearing gifts. Do precisely as you are bid.*

Bracknell went back to the window and saw the retired sailor, his face darkened from many summers upon the seas, staring up at his chamber. The old man then did something that startled Bracknell, for he took his pocket watch from his waistcoat pocket, popped the silver lid open, and with a handkerchief, wiped the glass face of the watch.

Bracknell was shocked, rooted to the floor. It couldn't be! There was only one man of Bracknell's acquaintance who had ever used such a signal—Vincent Warfield.

The sailor smiled, tipped his hat, and moved on. Was it Vincent? Of course it was! Everything made sense now.

Bracknell's first thought was that Ellen would be struck to the very core of her being at the knowledge that her father was still alive. He knew she had grieved terribly for Vincent. How would she receive the knowledge that his death had been a ruse, a very clever scheme to expose his nephew.

He realized many things at once. Vincent had protected his daughter throughout, keeping Becky, who was surely working for him as well, close at hand to watch over Ellen, and even—the matchmaking old fool!—by providing her with a husband.

Reading the note again, Bracknell interpreted the last sentence to mean he was to go without firearms, *in a friendly manner*, and to bring the coded articles with him, *bearing gifts*. Gathering the fan, the snuffbox, and the kerchief, he slapped his beaver hat on his head and quit his room.

Ellen sat before a delicate nuncheon served on a table set with fine Irish linen. But never had cold chicken seemed less appetizing than in this moments. Her husband, her love, would die, and it was her fault. Yet not her fault, for he was a despicable spy. But somehow it didn't matter, to her what he was. She loved him, and the mere thought of having to live without him hurt so badly, her chest felt as though it might cave in on her if she took a deep breath. Surely there was something she could do. But how could she help him? It was too late.

Her thoughts turned sharply to her sister, and she wondered whether Celeste and Jeremy and the boys had reached Scotland, and whether or not her sister was still content with her decision. What would Celeste do in this fix? Would Celeste make an effort to rescue her love and perhaps flee the country?

Ellen let the fork clatter to her plate as she pushed herself back from the table. Rising to her feet, she tried to picture what sort of life she would have at Warfield Hall—long winter nights, empty summer days—and somehow she knew she would never find such a love again. With a sinking sensation she realized Lord Bracknell was truly a very unique sort of man, much as her papa had been.

Just like her papa. A little flicker of light glimmered in her brain. Lord Bracknell had been to see her father two weeks before he died. And that had not been the first time. No, their friendship had been of long standing. What had Bracknell said? Ten years.

She stepped over to the window, the wheels of her imagination beginning to spin. Becky had given her a hint: "You ain't got the sense to figure out what's going on beneath your own short, stubby little nose." She reached up and touched her nose again, then separated the lace curtains to peer down into the busy street. A cloaked figure, carrying a cane, hurried across the street toward the inn and narrowly escaped being run over by a stanhope gig. His hat fell off in the process, and Ellen was startled to see it was Ambrose when he scrambled to his feet, raising an angry fist to the driver of the gig. But, of course, Ambrose had said he would be here, that he would do all he could to effect Bracknell's capture.

Her heart began to pound. Ambrose had always been a liar; even when he was very small he had told a whisker that earned Ellen a thrashing she didn't deserve. She backed away from the window, comprehension flooding her mind with a horror so great, she wanted to crawl beneath the bed and hide forever. Bracknell wasn't selling secrets to the French: it was Ambrose. Bracknell had been working with her father before he died, her father, who was great friends with the Duke of York and with the Prince Regent.

Oh, God, no! That, explained why the men had all looked so uncomfortable at the navy office, clearing their throats and scuffling their feet. How foolish she felt suddenly. She was so confused. What should she do? Was Ambrose coming here? Did he mean to do her harm? Oh, why had she not seen it all before?

A rapping sounded on her door, and her heart thudded against her ribs. "Who is it?" she called out.

"Your beloved cousin, of course. Open the door. I have something urgent to tell you."

"I am indisposed. I . . . I am quite ill and cannot receive visitors of the moment."

The doorknob twisted slightly. Thank god she had locked the door. Silence ensued and she waited, her eyes fixed upon the knob. When would Becky return?

Suddenly the door slammed open; Ambrose flew into the room and immediately thrust the door shut behind him. His eyes were glittering with excitement as he lifted his cane to her and slid the blade from its sheath. "If you dare scream," he whispered, "I shall cut you to ribbons first and then expose your husband to my very good friends here. They will know precisely what to do with him. I assure you they are experts."

Ellen trembled all over, her gaze watching the light from the window glint upon the polished steel of the blade.

He relaxed his arm slightly. "I mean to have the Hall as well as the fortune for your father's cleverly coded articles. Vincent meant to entrap me, you know."

Ellen shook her head. "I didn't know. I didn't know anything. I was so certain it was Hugh. How could I have been so blind, so stupid? You are the traitor, Ambrose! You have betrayed England!" And she pointed at him, her arm trembling.

"You always were willing to believe the wrong things of the wrong people. Your judgment was never acute."

She tried to control the sense of panic that threatened to consume her. She concentrated on his features instead. His white cheeks were flushed in odd little patches, and his green-gold eyes were cold and harsh. "What do you mean to do?"

"First we must find your *husband*, and then I shall see that you both get what you deserve. My French friends no doubt will do anything I require."

Once outside the inn, Ellen tried to pull away from Ambrose, but he gripped her arm in a surprisingly strong grasp, and she could not break free. He whispered, "I learned a very interesting method of breaking limbs when I first began this business four years ago. The Frenchies tested me several times. And once they broke my wrist. I hope they shall do the same to Lord Bracknell."

Ellen felt faint, her knees buckling slightly. How very right she had been about Ambrose. He would do anything to achieve his ends. A post chaise pulled forward, and the door flew open. Within the coach Ellen saw her maid, and she cried "Becky, help me!" a momentary feeling of relief washing over her. But something was wrong.

As Ambrose forced her into the coach Becky lifted her brow and spoke caustically, "Help you do what, Miss

Ellen? Change your undergarments?" And she laughed loudly, sounding quite like an old witch cackling over her pot of brew. "You may give me your emerald ring, for you won't be needing it where you're going." She laughed again.

"What does this mean?" Ellen whispered, as Becky grasped her hand and jerked the ring off her finger. She did not want an answer, for it was obvious her maid had joined ranks with Ambrose, or had she? Becky delivering messages, Becky disappearing for stretches at a time, Becky never giving her ground, but treating her as harshly as her father had. She truly did not know what to think.

She leaned back into the squabs and pretended to weep. "Pray let me go, Ambrose." she pleaded. "What have I done to you?"

"Do stop sniveling, Cousin. It doesn't become you."

"I'm frightened!"

Becky said, "I told you not to marry Bracknell. All would have been well had you just stayed in London. But you were always headstrong."

When Ambrose turned his head for a moment to look out the window, Becky winked at her and gave her a very stern, serious nod. Ellen knew then that whatever was going forward, Becky was not in league with Ambrose.

In a few moments they pulled in front of a red-brick house of large proportions with a model ship in one of the front windows. A moment later they were inside, Ambrose having asked for a man by the name of Charles. As they entered the drawing room Ellen immediately saw Lord Bracknell seated in front of a desk, blood dripping from his mouth, his hands apparently tied behind him. "Hugh!" she cried, and ran to him, "What have they done to you? Oh, my dearest love, I have been wrong about so many things —I only learned of it too late. It was my cousin who was involved with . . . with these evil men."

Only then did she look up and glance at the men about the desk. Two looked vaguely familiar to her, and with a start she realized that only that morning she had seen them at the navy office. Her shock was so great that, lest she give anything away, she buried her face in Bracknell's coat sleeve and again pretended to cry. She did not understand what was happening, but something desperate was in the works, and she knew if she was not very careful, she had the power to ruin it all. Real tears, tears of sheer fright, made their way to her eyes as she lifted her face to gaze at her husband.

With trembling fingers she took a kerchief from her reticule and dabbed at the blood on his face. And as she wiped gently the red streak smeared oddly. Stage makeup. Lifting her gaze to meet his, she saw the warning light in his eyes, and she knew a terrible need to remain very, very silent.

Ambrose sauntered into the room and greeted two of the men, who smiled happily upon him. One of them, a tall, thin man with a black mustache, said, "You have just given us all the proof we need. I take it this man," and he leveled his hand toward Bracknell, "is an impostor."

Ambrose laughed, swinging his cane. "What a clever choice of words. But, yes, as it happens, I had the truth from my contact in London—he is an English agent and was sent here to entrap all of you." He moved toward the desk and saw the telegraph fan, the kerchief, and the snuffbox sitting there. "I see he has brought Ellen's trifles. How very efficient," he said as he turned toward the viscount. "And how very stupid to come here alone, Bracknell." He rapped his cane against the viscount's boot, and Ellen drew in her breath, her gaze fixed on the handle of the cane, trembling clear to her toes.

He then addressed the man with the black mustache. "But since I have helped confirm your suspicions and saved you from exposure, I trust you will relinquish your treasure into my care." He tapped on the leather valise sitting atop the desk next to Ellen's possessions. "I assure you the coded information delivered to you today is worth every tuppence."

One of the men familiar to Ellen handed him the leather case, and Ambrose did not hesitate to open it. From where Ellen was kneeling beside Bracknell she could see into the case and was astonished at the sight of so many pound notes.

The mustachioed man laughed brightly and said, "Quite a fortune there, more than even the packet last year. Do you remember that lark, Hazeley? Faith, I did not think I would make it beyond Spithead."

Ellen saw the small movements—a slight shift of the gaze there, a twitch of the finger here—as the room grew strangely quiet. Waiting.

"Do I remember it! My god, I had the devil of a time convincing Jack here," and he gestured to the rather plain-faced man whom he had greeted earlier, "that the packet was genuine." His words trailed off as he looked around, awareness flooding him.

As fast as a whip he reached down and caught Ellen beneath her arm, forcing her to stand next to him. He had drawn the blade from the handle of his cane, the remainder of the mahogany stick falling with a dull thump to the carpet, and now pressed the knife to her throat. "No!" she cried.

Bracknell was on his feet, but Hazeley held Ellen about her waist and was dragging her backward. "Just stay where you are, and she won't get hurt. I will promise you that."

Something bumped against Ellen's hip, and she realized Ambrose held the leather valise with the same hand he was using to hold her. He could commandeer his own ship for that price.

Ellen hurt in every part of her body, her muscles aching with fear. If he were but to trip, she would be dead.

A voice that sounded strangely familiar spoke from behind them. "Let her go, Ambrose, or I shall be forced to pull the trigger of this neat little pistol of mine."

"Warfield!" Ambrose cried. And because he was stunned by the sound of Vincent's voice, his arm dropped away from Ellen.

Ellen tumbled to the carpeted floor and looked up to see not her father but the old sailor Becky had been flirting with. She looked at him hard, at the clearness of his one unpatched blue eye. It was not her father, or was it? The man's face was dark, burned by years in the sun aboard a sailing vessel. He even walked with that peculiar swagger of sailing men, as though he were balancing the sea beneath his boots. It was only someone who sounded like her father, surely.

She felt Bracknell's hand at her elbow as she rose to her feet, but she did not turn even to look at him. She could not tear her eyes from the old man, nor could Ambrose. It was too unreal!

Bracknell moved swiftly across the room and caught Ambrose from behind, knocking the knife from his grasp and locking his arms behind his head. Then the room broke into a whirlwind of motion as the rest of the men rushed from about the desk and bound her cousin. He did not try to struggle, his face growing white as he realized how thoroughly he had been entrapped.

He said to the sailor, "It was you from the start, wasn't it, Uncle?"

The old man nodded as they hauled Ambrose back to the desk and forced him to sit where Bracknell had been seated moments earlier. The sailor turned his attention to Ellen as he removed the patch from his eye. Even the swagger disappeared as he approached her and consoled, "I'm sorry, kitten. But I only did what had to be done under these terrible circumstances."

Chapter Fourteen

ELLEN STOOD FACING her father and trembled all over. She felt Becky's soothing presence as her maid slipped an arm about her shoulders and took her to a settee by the fireplace.

"Why didn't anyone tell me?" Her disbelieving gaze was still fixed firmly upon her papa. Turning to regard her maid, she cried, "Becky, you should have told me! Did you know from the first?"

Becky nodded and as she spoke Ellen realized her common dialect had disappeared entirely. "More than that, Miss Ellen. I've worked for your father for ten years now. I . . . I was an actress before that."

"Oh, no," Ellen cried, holding her hand to her cheek.

"Yes. I thought you knew everything not two days ago when you wondered at my not being an actress." And Becky reached down to press Ellen's emerald ring into her hand.

Ellen frowned at it, hardly aware what it was. Glancing up at Becky, she said, "Why, you do indeed have a lovely voice. And to think, all this time—Oh, but this is terrible. I feel so foolish, so stupid, so—so furious!"

She turned to look at her father again. "How could you?" Ellen cried, her voice causing every pair of eyes to glance sharply at her.

"That's enough of your temper, Ellen. Please, come into the library, and I'll tell you everything."

Ellen rose to her feet, still shaken from her misadventure, and was relieved to find Bracknell suddenly beside her, supporting her arm. To him, she said, "And I suppose you knew everything, too, you cur, you dog in the manger!"

He smiled softly at her. "No. I am sorry to disappoint you, but I believed your father dead as well."

The wind taken from her sails, the four of them proceeded to the library, where Vincent passed out glasses of sherry. He then removed his blue coat and belcher kerchief, and only when Ellen saw how white his neck was, did she realize his face had been stained. He caught her surprised expression and said, "The juice of walnuts. I'm told it will fade in time."

Ellen sat down on a chair by the desk and sipped her sherry. "But why, Papa?" she asked finally.

Regarding his daughter squarely, Vincent perched himself on the edge of the desk. "I knew you and Bracknell both so well. And you were as spoiled and heartless a female as I'd ever known!"

"Papa!"

Vincent lifted a hand and continued, "Don't eat me, my pet! I love you, but what did you know of men or of love? Naught. And you were so determined to remain a spinster. I've never told you this, but shortly before your mother died, she gave me a difficult task to perform. Faith, I remember it all so clearly." His blue eyes appeared clouded as he swallowed hard. "You were only a little girl then, but she seemed to know what you were. 'Vincent, see that Ellen marries,' she said. 'She talks incessantly of being just like Queen Elizabeth. And I know her—the stubborn girl she is, she's already decided. And the worst of it is, she will never know what she has given up.'

"You had the toughest shell about you—and for four years, since you were first come out, I watched you repulse every gentleman who got within a yard of your heart. Why, you even dressed like the Virgin Queen at every masquerade! Except the one to Vauxhall, of course. I never thought to see one of my daughters dressed like . . . like . . . "

He was apparently quite shocked, and Ellen cried, "You were there?" She pressed her hands to her cheeks at the sudden memory of the Grecian gown.

"Yes, I went as a cow. The most unbearable costume!"

"The cow!" Ellen cried. "I remember you!"

Lord Bracknell said, "And Becky was there as well."

Ellen turned to her maid with an inquiring expression.

Becky answered gaily, laughing, "Yes, and I never had so much fun in my life—your papa was so upset by your costume!"

Ellen opened her eyes wide. "Not—not Cleopatra!" As Becky nodded, Ellen rubbed her forehead wondering what she would hear next.

Vincent addressed the viscount: "You must forgive an old man, Hugh, but here it is—I knew you to be just about as thick-sculled as my daughter here. I never told you this, but I saw you both at the opera a year ago. And if ever two people, spoiled by society's pandering, deserved each other, it was you and Ellen."

Bracknell interjected, "Say no more. I now consider myself in your debt. We are married, you know."

Vincent slapped his hands against his legs and laughed. "You may come to regret it!"

To Ellen he said, "I knew if the pair of you ever had reason to be together for even the smallest period of time, you'd discover each other. As it happens, I was right." And he smiled brightly from one to the other. "But I always had two purposes in mind—one, to marry you to Bracknell if I could and the other, to entrap my nephew."

"Did Ambrose know of the will?" Ellen asked.

"Toward the end I had Becky tell him."

"Why?"

"To force him out. To force him to act. I couldn't be sure he wouldn't catch wind of the trap—and I was right about that: he did learn of it later—and I knew the business of the will would distract him completely. Avarice was always his real fault."

"But why did you feel you must pretend to die? Couldn't you have accomplished all of this and . . . and just pretended to be sailing to India or something?"

He rubbed his eyes and thought for a moment. "I wanted Hazeley to believe that with a little manipulation, he could win the estate. I knew him. I knew he had always felt cheated out of the property, even though it was never his, never! And after he stole your sister's portion—damme, I'm angry all over again just thinking about it!" He was quiet for a moment, composing himself, then finally added, "Besides, I wanted to force your hand as well!"

Bracknell asked, "And were you at the Fountain, sir, when Ellen—er—abducted me?"

He smiled with satisfaction. "Yes, and I have never been so entertained in all my life. I suppose you heard me laughing."

"And afterward you fell into a fit of coughing. The odd thing was, your laughter sounded vaguely familiar, but I couldn't place it."

Ellen spoke quietly: "I remember it, too, though I still had no idea—" She could not keep from staring at her father. He was a ghost, surely, and if she rubbed her eyes, he would disappear into the paneling behind the walnut desk upon which he was sitting. How serene he appeared as he regarded her, his blue eyes filled with love. Suddenly she was overcome with so much emotion, she leapt to her feet and threw herself into his arms. "Papa!" she cried, tears overflowing onto his neck. "Oh, Papa, you've come back!"

He held her fiercely, and whispered, "I know it was a very cruel thing to do, but I saw no other way. I'm sorry. And look what I've done. I've spilled sherry on your pelisse."

"I don't care one whit. You may drench my entire person in sherry for all I care! Oh, how good it is to have you here!" She clung to him for a long time, unable to say more. When she could speak again, she regarded him solemnly and said, "Celeste has eloped to Scotland with Jeremy Andover."

He didn't say anything for a moment, and when he did

speak, his voice was low with emotion. "I am sorry to hear it, but I'm not surprised. Poor Celly! I should have had her marriage to Ambrose annulled the second they returned from Gretna. But you know what your sister was then: she would simply have run off with him again. Still, to think he—"

He couldn't continue, but moved to a chair by the window and pulled her onto his lap. "I've thought a thousand times about what should happen next, and I still haven't decided. You see, the Duke of York discovered Hazeley's treachery a full year ago, but he used him for a time, feeding the Frenchies false information, and finally gave me this opportunity to deal with my nephew in my own way—without a scandal, if possible. There are the boys to consider, you see, my grandsons. And these men . . ."—he gestured toward the door that lead to the drawing room—"are all sworn to secrecy; perfectly reliable, too. But it can't end here. I just don't know what to do. If I turn Ambrose over to the authorities, there'll be a public outcry so great, even the boys will find a social life impossible for many years to come. I could have Ambrose perform a gentlemanly suicide, but we would still be left with a body to explain away."

Becky, who had been sipping her sherry and listening intently to this exchange, suggested, "I understand a convict ship heading for New South Wales is more than enough punishment for any crime. And if a small yachting party were arranged, and Ambrose tumbled overboard . . ."

Ellen viewed her father and inquired, "What do you think, Papa? It would seem terribly ironic to let the world believe Ambrose died—as you let the world believe you died—and then send him to a penal colony."

"It violates several morals. The man should hang."

Ellen said, "I don't know what is right or wrong. I only know my sister has suffered enough."

This seemed to decide the matter, and Vincent said, "York left the decision up to me, but we did agree life imprisonment at New South Wales would be a fair measure of justice, perhaps more even than hanging, for a worse lot is not to be found than in such a place." He sighed heavily. "I think we shall arrange that yachting accident of yours, Becky. I see no other way. I just can't bring myself to heap any more pain upon Celeste or her children."

Ellen nestled her head in his shoulder and sighed. She was glad it was all over, that Ambrose would no longer be near to hurt anyone ever again, but mostly she was just grateful to have her father with her. With a start she realized that since her father was alive, there was no need to fulfill the terrible terms of his will. For a month all she had thought about was the will, and even though she understood the purpose of her father's schemes, she suddenly felt outraged again, and she leapt away from him as though she had just discovered she was sitting upon a hot coal.

"Papa!" she cried. "How could you? Your will! That man!" she gestured wildly to Bracknell. "You—you tricked me!"

Vincent regarded his daughter with a satisfied smile on his face. "I wasn't sure I could do it, but I thought it might just work out, and damme, here I am staring at Lady Bracknell!"

"No," she cried. "Never! I have been tricked and deceived by—by both of you!" She whirled to face her husband. "And you—how could you let me believe you were a spy? You don't know all the horrible things I thought about you."

He said quietly, "And I hoped you would trust more in my character."

This softened her a little, and she said, "I did, toward the end, just before Ambrose beat my door down." She felt so confused. "Only then did I realize which of you was the traitor."

Bracknell set his glass of sherry on a table by his chair, and rose, saying, "And I am heartily glad to hear it."

She watched his approach, fear striking her heart. She had forced him to marry her, and a thousand thoughts whirled about her brain. She spoke some of them aloud: "You don't love me. I held a pistol to your head. That is why you married me."

He took her in his arms. "My dear, I daresay you didn't notice, but the flint in the flintlock was missing. Even if you had properly tamped the powder into the pistol, it could not have discharged. You coerced me into nothing."

"Then you knew from the start I was, for all intents and purposes, unarmed?"

Vincent gave a shout of laughter and interjected, "I warned you to become knowledgeable about my pistols, Ellen."

She ignored her father, feeling quite hurt in some hidden place of her heart. She said, "Then you married me because you are deeply in debt?" She stared at the folds of his neckcloth, where the false blood had stained the white linen.

He lifted her chin, forcing her to meet his gaze, and said, "Again, I will have to disappoint you. My own fortune is comfortably intact."

"You have not mortgaged Three Elms?"

"I would sell my soul first."

Ellen nodded at this, comprehending his sentiments perfectly.

"Besides, I had to marry you, or have you forgotten you are going to have a baby, though whose child it is will be something we will have to discuss at length."

"A baby!" Vincent cried.

Bracknell said, "I shall explain that to you at a later date." Laughing, he addressed Ellen: "Besides, my dear, though I have a tidy fortune, you are amazingly wealthy, or will be once your father really does decide to pay his debt to nature, and I had always hoped to marry an heiress. One can never have enough of the ready, you know!"

"You are a beast!" she cried, feeling considerably relieved at his bantering tone. "How can you speak about my father in that horrid manner?" Offering her husband a tremulous smile as she leaned into him, she continued, "And I thought I had prepared the pistol with such skill! I'd no idea." She pulled on the lapel of his coat, only vaguely aware that the door had snapped shut behind her father and

Becky. She asked, "Then—then, are you saying you love me?"

"Well, I would not go quite that far. I tolerate you. You are uncommonly spoiled, you know."

"I know, but I mean to do better," she said in a quiet voice, and turned her face up to him so she soon had all the pleasure of again finding herself lost in his embrace. All the tension of the last few weeks fled her body as he kissed her gently. Ambrose would be gone forever, and her father would be home to dandle his grandchildren upon his knee.

Three days later Ellen sat in the large morning room at Warfield Hall with two newspapers spread out before her, *The Times* and *The Morning Post*. She giggled over the fine account of her father's remarkable reappearance after having been stranded for six months upon a nameless island somewhere in the Channel just off the coast of France. The article went on to say that he would be spending the rest of the year tucked safely within the bosom of his family.

She turned to her husband, who was just finishing a cup of coffee and said, "What a sham. I only saw him on Saturday at Portsmouth, and then only once in the morning on Sunday. Do you know that as soon as he had greeted the servants here, he put his hat on his head, told me to enjoy my honeymoon, and then left to join the Prince Regent in Brighton? The bosom of his family, indeed!"

"It is all my fault. I hinted him away. It is our honeymoon after all."

Ellen sniffed, "It wouldn't have mattered one whit. Had I been unwed, he would merely have kissed me once on the cheek, asked me why I was not in London, and then left for Brighton anyway."

He said, "You sound very unhappy. I must do something about that." His gaze swept over her hair, and she could see a familiar desire take hold of him. Releasing the newspapers, she leaned over to him and kissed him full on the mouth. But this was something of a mistake, for he pulled her bodily from her chair and drew her onto his lap, ignoring her protests that the servants might walk in or that it was but eleven in the morning or that she had just completed her toilette. And she hoped he would never stop.

But a feminine voice intruded. "Ellen, what are you doing!"

Ellen jumped from Bracknell's lap, forgetting for a moment she was married to the wicked rake, and patting her curls, cried, "Celly! Oh, my dear, you've come home!"

Within seconds the sisters were embracing. Celeste wept into her kerchief and poured out her story, while Jeremy stood frowning in the background. She told Ellen the newspapers had carried the story of Ambrose's death in a yachting accident, and then today she and Jeremy had read of her father's miraculous rescue. They had not been to Scotland, but had gotten stuck somewhere near York—Marcus had taken a chill and they felt it wiser to stay there—so of course they had returned immediately.

Ellen held her sister close. She and her father had agreed Celeste would never know the truth. Her sister's sobs hurt Ellen terribly as she led her to a small sofa by the fireplace. "Pray, don't cry, my dear! You should be very happy!"

"I cannot believe he is gone," Celeste said, blowing her nose. "It must have happened very soon after—after we—that is—"

Ellen knelt beside her and held her hand tightly. "It was all very tragic, dearest, but he is gone. And you must think now of Julian and Marcus. Don't feel sad for Ambrose."

Celeste cried, "But that is the worst of it. I am glad he is gone! I am happy his days have ended and his sons won't have to know what their father was. I am a hateful person to be so relieved, to be happy Ambrose is—is—" And she cried even harder.

Jeremy moved to stand by Celeste and placed his hand gently upon her shoulder. He addressed Ellen: "She has been inconsolable." His own dark eyes were grief-stricken. "She refuses to marry me now that she is free. She keeps saying something foolish about being unworthy—" He broke off, running a hand through his wild hair, and moved impatiently toward the fireplace.

Ellen pressed her sister's hand hard and wondered what she should say. Finally she concluded that a bit of distraction might serve the purpose. "Well, Celly, I hope, then, you shall be happy for me, because I married Hugh, not three days ago, in Portsmouth."

Celeste stopped crying immediately, and with a kerchief pressed to her nose, looked up at Ellen and said, "Truly? Oh, my dear, what wonderful tidings." She was on her feet instantly, hugging Ellen, then racing to the table to give Bracknell a sisterly kiss upon his cheek, vowing now they would all be as happy as clams and, oh, life would be so wonderful! And asking when would it be proper to place a notice in *The Morning Post* announcing her engagement to Jeremy and if Ellen thought this time she might be married in church?

Stealing a glance at the poet, Ellen laughed at his confused expression, for he apparently did not know what to make of Celeste's abrupt change of mood. Ellen took pity on him, and slipping an arm through his, drew him to the dining table, where she forced him to sit and partake of a little coffee. Bracknell lifted his cup to Ellen in a silent toast, and Celeste cried, "So, what did Papa say to my having eloped with Jeremy? I would have enjoyed seeing the shock on his face. It is only a little of what he deserves for having tortured us with his dreadful schemes for so long, and for actually arranging his own demise. That is, not his death, but pretending to be dead, which is just as bad. . . ."

Ellen did not try to answer her, but merely smiled at the return of her sister's spirits. She blew a kiss across the table to her husband, and in the drive she could hear Huntley, the head groom, his boots crunching on the gravel, as he called after Julian and Marcus, "Return those bridles at once!"

The sunlight drifted over the lime trees along the avenue, and Ellen thought that the spring of 1812 would forever be the sweetest season throughout all her life.